HER LOYAL PROTECTOR

A Strong Family Romance Companion Novel

CAMI CHECKETTS

Birch River
PUBLISHING

FREE BOOK

Sign up for Cami's VIP newsletter and receive a free ebook copy of *The Resilient One: A Billionaire Bride Pact Romance* here.

You can also receive a free copy of *Rescued by Love: Park City Firefighter Romance* by clicking here and signing up for Cami's newsletter.

CHAPTER ONE

Kaytlyn Klein rushed through the wide halls of Jacob Tarbet's mansion. She'd worked for Jacob for almost ten years now, though for the past five he'd treated her more like a partner than an employee. He'd found her waiting tables in his hometown of Sun Valley, where she'd been scraping by just trying to earn enough money to ski on the weekends. Jacob had become a regular customer. Then he'd seen her buying lunch for a family whose child had just been diagnosed with leukemia. He hired her as his personal assistant on the spot, paid for her online bachelor's degree in business, and taught her how to run his businesses and how to be poised and classy. He was the smartest, most generous, and most selfless person she knew.

Jacob and his daughter, Jessica, were Kaytlyn's closest friends. Horrifically, Jacob was dying. Kaytlyn was also expecting Jessica's baby, a surrogate for Jessica and her husband, Peter. It still felt foreign to be pregnant and she touched her abdomen, awed that a small life rested inside. She knew she'd be attached to the little one, like a favorite aunt, but she found herself wishing, and sometimes believing, it was her own baby she carried. She forced those thoughts away quickly when she had them. What a blessing it was for Kaytlyn to be able to help someone she loved so much achieve their goal of being a mother.

As she approached Jacob's suite, she startled when a man stepped forward from the nook of the suite's doorframe, his handsome face lit with a soft smile. Her heart pounded so hard, she worried she would have heart failure and this fabulous specimen of a man would have to resuscitate her. She smiled to herself. Not a bad idea at all.

"Good morning, Cameron," she said, winking at him. She loved to tease the ever-tough military man, and she was happy that she could still tease despite the heaviness pressing down on her. Cameron was serious and dedicated to his job of protecting Jacob, but there was a mischievous glint in his eyes that intensified when he met Kaytlyn's gaze. She'd heard a couple of funny quips slip past his lips too, and if she could get him away from his protection detail, he might be really fun. For almost two years now, she'd been deftly flirting with him, but he hadn't asked her out ... yet.

"Morning, Kaytlyn." His too-blue eyes drew her in, and she stopped in front of him instead of hurrying into Jacob's suite to check in with her boss as she did every morning. "I've been thinking."

"Dangerous pastime," she joked.

He grinned. "I've got plenty of those. I'm hoping I can add another."

"What's that?"

"Taking you to dinner tonight."

Kaytlyn bit at her lip and tilted her head. Her long blond hair slid across her shoulder. "That might be dangerous for me," she kept her tone teasing so he'd know she admired his well-built body and wasn't afraid of him. She wanted to go to dinner with him, badly. She was only a month along and wouldn't show for a while now. Would Cameron think she was crazy to carry her friend's child or would he think it was admirable? Would he still want to date her when she started showing?

"No, I'd be the only one in danger." He lowered his voice and murmured, "Of losing my heart."

Kaytlyn's own heart thudded wildly. She couldn't believe this tough military man had just said that. Instead of admitting that she was already much too invested in him, she said, "I don't know nearly enough about you."

Cameron's eyebrows rose. "You hired me. I'd think you know plenty about me."

She had indeed hired him and four other ex-military security specialists from an entity out of California run by philanthropist Sutton Smith. While the men were all tough and competent, only Cameron had drawn her eye in the past two years; he tried to stay in the shadows when he was on duty to protect her billionaire boss, yet she never failed to notice him. Cameron's presence was larger than life, from his well-built body to the strong, handsome planes of his face to the intelligent, humorous spark in his blue eyes. He couldn't hide in the shadows, nor anywhere else. Though he was a soldier through and through, it was obvious that he was meant to be a leader.

"I know you graduated from West Point, spent almost ten years in the Army, took two tours in Afghanistan and one in Kuwait, and achieved the rank of sergeant before you retired three years ago and started working for Sutton Smith."

Cameron nodded, as stoic as ever, but there was a welcoming light in his blue eyes. "See? You know plenty about me."

"Do I?" She took a large step closer. She knew Cameron was trustworthy—the fact that her body automatically drew toward him was proof.

He didn't step back, instead leaning a little closer. He was interested. Yes! She hadn't dated much since high school graduation, choosing to work hard and spend her free time on the slopes in the winter and hiking in the summer. She'd gone on dates sometimes and traveled the world with Jacob, but no man had really caught her eye until she hired Cameron.

Kaytlyn said, "I don't know what your favorite food is, where your family lives, what sports you like to play, or what you like to do on dates."

A smile played around Cameron's lips, and his eyes were dancing. "How are you going to find out those things?"

She breathed in deeply; she was close enough that she could smell his clean, crisp scent. "When we go to dinner tonight, I'll be able to ask all kinds of questions."

Cameron's smile lit up his face, and Kaytlyn's eyes widened. She'd always thought he was handsome. When his full smile came out, he was the most irresistibly appealing man she'd ever come across.

"Six?" was all he asked, but that smile told her everything she needed to know.

"Yes, sir." She mockingly saluted him.

"Wear your hiking clothes," he murmured, his gaze tracing across her face and warming her up from the inside out.

Yet again, she was impressed. He'd noticed that her favorite pastime was exploring the mountain trails close to their home. It was early July, and the trails in the mountains around Sun Valley were insanely beautiful, exploding with greenery and wildflowers.

Her phone rang Jacob's tone, and she reluctantly stepped back and pulled it out of her purse. "Yes?" she answered, grinning at Cameron. They were going on a date. She'd said yes. Maybe tonight she could tell him about the little one inside of her. She thought he'd take it superbly. She was excited to spend one on one time with this intriguing man.

"When you come this morning ..." Jacob sounded more tired than usual, as if it was an obvious effort to talk. Had he taken a turn for the worse? Her heart ached at the thought. "Bring Cameron in."

"Okay. I'm here." She ended the phone call and slid it back into her purse. "He wants both of us to come in."

Cameron's eyes asked the question, but his military training was strong enough that he didn't put voice to it. She didn't have answers anyway, so she just moved toward the door to open it. Cameron moved in front of her, and his strong arm brushed against hers. Warmth spread through her as his eyes shot to hers again. Did he feel the connection as strongly as she did? After she met with Jacob about work questions and ideas, she was going to tell him that she and Cameron were going to start dating. She doubted her friend would have any objections, but she wanted to make sure she was up front with the man who had done so much for her.

Cameron pushed the door open, then stepped back to let her walk through. Kaytlyn gave him an unsteady smile and walked briskly into the suite. The nurses had already been here; Jacob liked them to come early. Jacob was sitting up in bed, dressed in a golf polo and comfortable sweats, as ready for the day as he could be. The retractable blinds were open, giving an incredible view of the lush mountain valley, green and sparkling in the early-morning sun.

"Come in, come in." Jacob gestured to both of them, surprisingly energetic, as if their presence granted him strength. Kaytlyn knew he and Cameron had grown close over the past two years, and she imagined Cameron felt as much respect for Jacob as she did.

Kaytlyn's heels tapped across the hardwood floor as she approached the bed. Cameron was by her side. He stopped a few feet away, but Kaytlyn walked right up to the bed. Jacob extended his hand, and she clasped his fingers with her own. He was only in his early sixties, but the battle with bone marrow cancer made him look like he was eighty.

"How are you this morning, Kayt?" He wasn't himself. She couldn't put a finger on it, but something was troubling him deeply.

"Wonderful." It was true. She was going out with Cameron. "Have you been giving the nurses a hard time?"

He waved his free hand and gave her a half of a smile. "Always. I'm so happy you're here."

Maybe it was his time and he knew it. She wasn't ready for that, and she doubted she'd ever be.

"You look beautiful today," Jacob continued. "What am I saying? You look beautiful every day. A face like an angel." His smile grew and he patted her hand, as if he were a proud uncle, not just her best friend. "Am I right, Cameron?"

Kaytlyn glanced back at Cameron, who was watching the two of them steadily. Cameron nodded, warming her face with his blue gaze. "Yes, sir."

Jacob gestured to Cameron. "Bring some chairs over, will you, son? I've got something important to discuss with Kaytlyn, and I want you to be our witness."

Kaytlyn's pulse sped up. She knew it. Something was going on, something out of the ordinary. They discussed important matters every day: his investments, his numerous businesses, and the charitable foundation they'd dreamed up together, Protect the Young. She couldn't help putting a hand to her abdomen. There was a little one growing within her. No matter that he wasn't hers, she already loved the child. It was perfect that it was

Jessica's, if only Peter didn't make Kaytlyn so uncomfortable with his comments and lewd looks.

Cameron slid a chair up for her. She thanked him and sat close to Jacob's bedside.

"You too," Jacob said.

Cameron retrieved his own chair and set it next to Kaytlyn's. His strong presence so close was messing with her brain waves, but she simply set her large purse on the floor and pulled her laptop out. "What's on the agenda for today, boss?" she asked. Each of Jacob's businesses, from the restaurants to the theaters to the ski resorts, had more-than-competent managers, but Jacob still liked to be involved and Kaytlyn was basically in charge of everything now. When he passed, it would be hard to turn everything over Jessica and Peter. Even Protect the Young. Kaytlyn felt like she was part of the family but she was still an employee, and didn't own any of it. Jessica had promised they'd keep her involved.

"Something ... tough," Jacob murmured. His eyes darted to her abdomen then back up again. "Put the laptop away. I need you to focus on me."

Kaytlyn's hand trembled on the laptop. Jacob had never asked her to put it away. She glanced at Cameron but he looked as confused as she felt. What was going on?

CHAPTER TWO

Kaytlyn did as instructed, sliding the laptop back in her purse. She sat straight in the chair and gave Jacob her full attention.

He reached for her hand again. "Kaytlyn. You've been like the daughter I always wanted and the best friend any old man could ask for."

She squeezed his hand, a little confused. Jessica was his daughter. She and Kaytlyn had grown close throughout the years, despite Jessica getting irritable and oddly jealous of Kaytlyn at times. When Jessica couldn't conceive a baby, Kaytlyn hadn't hesitated when she and Peter asked her to be their surrogate. She wasn't comfortable around Peter, but she loved Jessica.

Yet Jessica had acted really off the few times they'd texted or chatted on the phone the past four weeks. Kaytlyn worried Jessica was upset and envious that Kaytlyn got to experience the pregnancy she wanted so badly. Yet Jessica was busy supporting her husband who was a state senator hoping to move on to the U.S. Senate and someday become president. That was why Kaytlyn hadn't had a chance to have a heart-to-heart with her and make sure everything was all right with her friend.

"Thank you, Jacob," Kaytlyn said. "You're my best friend as well. Thank you for seeing the potential in me and giving me so much." Without him she'd be on the streets.

She could feel how stiff and uncomfortable Cameron was beside her. He was probably wondering why he was here to witness them gushing about each other. If he knew about her pregnancy, would he rescind his date offer?

"Now. I have something to ask of you, something ... huge. Please understand you can tell me no."

Kaytlyn couldn't remember ever telling Jacob no. He'd always been so good to her, and their relationship was as pure and undefiled as her love for her mother, her two younger sisters, and Jessica. "You know you can ask anything of me."

Jacob's dark eyes grew contemplative. "I hope so." He drew in a breath and said, "Jessica came to visit me last night."

Kaytlyn's gaze darted to Cameron, and he confirmed it with a nod. Cameron had been overseeing the safety and protection of the mansion and Jacob ever since a kidnapping and ransom attempt two years ago. When they used to go out in public, Cameron or one of the other bodyguards would be close by. Now that Jacob was homebound, the guards' job was much easier, but they were still here.

"Oh? What did she want?" She tried to say it positively but it stung. She thought Jessica was still in Boise. Why wouldn't her friend come and at least say hi? At least come check on her and the baby. The last time Kaytlyn had seen her was the day of the procedure in Boise. Kaytlyn had flown back to Sun Valley shortly after and Jessica had stayed to be with Peter.

He drew in a breath and pushed it out. "I changed my will recently."

"You did?" That was news to her but he could do anything he wanted with his money.

"I changed it to give you the foundation."

Kaytlyn's heart hammered faster. She glanced at Cameron who smiled gently at her. She'd asked Jacob to start the foundation about five years ago because she'd been neglected and emotionally abused by her father, and Jacob had supported her and helped her make the charity even better than she could imagine. Now, Protect the Young had orphanages and family and women's centers throughout the world, in addition to well-stocked food and supply pantries that were always available to parents and children in need.

"Thank you, Jacob." Her voice broke. She normally wasn't a crier but this was huge, and maybe there was something to be said for pregnancy hormones.

He nodded. "And I changed it to gift you with fifty million dollars. Fifty million that is already available or easy to liquidate."

"What?" Kaytlyn put a hand to her heart, hardly able to swallow. "I don't need ..." She couldn't think what to even say.

"I thought it would be enough for you to run the foundation, create other charities that I know you've wanted to create, and live happily." His eyes filled with sorrow and regret. "I thought with the gift you're giving to Peter and Jessica she would be ecstatic with the change in will."

Kaytlyn's stomach lurched uncomfortably. She put a hand to it. Cameron's eyes dipped to her hand and he gave her a questioning look. They hadn't told anyone about the pregnancy yet. She was hoping to have time alone with him at dinner to explain. Jessica had begged and Kaytlyn had so few close friends, of course she wanted to do this for Jessica and Jacob. Not for Peter so much. He made her uncomfortable, always complimenting her and giving her significant looks. She'd noticed Jessica didn't seem to like the way he treated her either, and Kaytlyn didn't blame her friend.

"Jessica threw a fit."

Kaytlyn shrugged, even though it hurt she wanted to write off the reaction. Jessica was intense. She was either happy or sad and some would say Jacob had spoiled her rotten, but Kaytlyn didn't allow that kind of talk about her friend. She'd seen Jessica throw her share of fits, but Kaytlyn's more even disposition was a good balance for Jessica's fun-loving but sometimes mad or irritated personality.

"She said ... a lot of things," Jacob continued.

"She was upset," Kaytlyn immediately defended Jessica and

honestly didn't want to hear the things. She was loyal to her friend. She was carrying her child.

"Ah, Kayt. You're always so kind." Jacob stared intently at her. "You have to hear what I am going to tell you."

Kaytlyn hesitated but then nodded. She could be strong. She'd been emotionally abused by her father for eighteen years. Pulled herself out fo that situation to become happy and successful. She could stand to hear that Jessica didn't want to share her fortune. Kaytlyn knew Jacob's finances. Fifty million that could be easily liquidated would be hard for Jessica to give up with Peter's political aspirations and propensity to spend. She about suggested he give her far less or restructure to give her a few of his businesses that were slow profit centers. She could manage them, just like she was already doing, and use excess profits to run her foundation.

"Kayt." He looked out the window. "She despises you."

"Excuse me?" Kaytlyn's back hit the chair. She turned to Cameron. He was staring compassionately at her, as if he already knew.

"It all came out last night." Jacob shook his head. "She said she's always been jealous of you—your beauty, your kindness, your brilliance at business. She feels like you took her place as my daughter and now she claims you're trying to steal Peter."

"What?" Kaytlyn's stomach rolled with disgust at that suggestion, and at the same time her heart broke that Jessica might truly despise her. Jealousy could turn ugly, she knew that, but why would Jessica accuse her of going after her too-smooth husband? Could her friend truly ... despise her?

"She said that you came to them offering to be their surrogate and apparently they used your egg because Jessica had none."

"What?" She shot to her feet, temporarily forgetting her angst over Jessica. If what Jacob had just said was true, it would help to explain why she already felt so attached to the tiny one growing inside her. Yet if it were true, she was carrying her and Peter's child? That made Kaytlyn so faint with repulsion she sank back into her seat.

"You're ... expecting?" Cameron asked, breaking his long silence. He looked so tough and protective of her. She wanted to lean against him for support, but forced herself to be strong and stay straight.

Kaytlyn nodded. "I thought I was carrying Peter and Jessica's baby." She turned back to Jacob. "Why would she tell you that?" She could hardly believe everything she was hearing. Jessica turning her back on Kaytlyn because of money and jealousy? Jessica hating her. Jessica claiming Kaytlyn had offered to be the surrogate when the truth was, Jessica had begged her. The most important thing right now seemed to be: The child growing within her might be ... Kaytlyn's? That was the only good news she'd heard this morning.

"You should've seen her. She was so upset it was like it all spilled out and then ... I assumed she'd cry and tell me she was sorry and beg me not to tell you, but ..." He looked away again. "I know I spoiled her, Kayt, but you know Jess, you love her too. I feel like Peter has broken her, twisted her mind and her perceptions. She didn't admit it, but I'm certain he's cheated on her. Now she's become bitter, selfish, and cruel. All she seems to care about are Peter's political ambitions, public perception, and her having everything she wants at any cost."

He rubbed at his brow. "I'm broken, Kayt. My girl." He shook his head. "The way she was so cold and unfeeling. I could feel how deep her hatred is for you, but also for ..." He broke off, cleared his throat, and started again, "For me."

Kaytlyn could understand, she felt broken too. Jacob had given Jessica all the love he could, losing his beloved wife when his daughter was only three. Kaytlyn and Jessica had grown very close the first few years Kaytlyn lived here. Things changed when Jessica married Peter, but Kaytlyn had buried her worries. She hadn't wanted to admit how much Jessica and their friendship had changed. She supposed now she could remember conniving or angry looks Jessica had given her, snide comments, but she'd written them off as Jessica just being in one of her moods. If Peter was stepping out on her ... that was horrible and made her feel some pity even though she could hardly believe Jessica could now despise her.

"She claimed she's going to destroy you, Kayt. She's going to take your baby, your fifty million, and bleed the foundation dry."

Kaytlyn could hardly catch a breath. Was this truly her baby? She placed her hand over her flat abdomen. The idea was thrilling and overwhelming. If it was true, she'd fight for her child with everything she had. She didn't care about the money, but she couldn't let anyone destroy the foundation. Too many children relied on and needed what her foundation provided.

"I think she honestly thought she'd throw her fit and I'd change my will back to her inheriting everything, but I saw through her last night, Kayt. She's dead inside now, only living to trample her way to the top."

Kaytlyn hated what he was saying. Could Jessica really have changed so much?

"I've heard rumors of how corrupt, and unfaithful, Peter is and recently Larry was able to confirm some of them through a private investigator he hired. I don't want that cheating liar having anything of mine. When they first married I thought he was sincere ... for about a year. Sadly it seems he and Jessica are both unethical and warped enough to believe that all that matters is their selfish ambitions. We've both loved Jessica, and I've given her everything I could her entire life, but I'm done now. Maybe the course I'm about to take will wake her up, but it might not." His gaze steadied on Kaytlyn and he nodded. "We're going to change my will ... again."

"You are?" Her eyes were drawn to Cameron as he shifted again. He was probably wondering why he was privy to this conversation. Jacob said he needed a witness. Why hadn't he called for his closest friend and lawyer, Larry?

"I've been on the phone with Larry last night and again this morning as more ideas and thoughts are stewing. He's currently doing the paperwork to immediately transfer all my resources, the businesses, and the foundation into your name and rewriting my will to reflect that. You're the sole beneficiary, Kayt."

Kaytlyn sucked in a breath, and she heard Cameron do the same next to her. Most people would probably be excited about the thought of becoming an instant billionaire, but Kaytlyn was only thinking about the responsibility. All those businesses and livelihoods, plus her foundation, would rely on her. Jacob had trained her well over the years, but it still was terrifying to think of doing it without him, and doing it while this baby grew inside her ... She placed a hand on her stomach. If it was true that they'd used Kaytlyn's egg without telling her, she could get genetic testing done, and she might be a single mother as well. There was no way she was sharing a baby with that vile Peter. He'd ruined her friend. He wasn't going to hurt her child.

"Please say yes, Kayt. There's no one else who I trust and who knows the businesses like you do. I hate to do this to my ... daughter." He had to clear his throat again. "But maybe if I'd done something tough years ago she wouldn't be so entitled and corrupt. The new will protects you, the foundation, and so many livelihoods. I know you'll do good things with the money. I wouldn't even be part of the foundation without you dreaming it all up."

She smiled, remembering. He'd been supportive but a little leery of giving so much money away, but she'd actually saved him a lot in taxes, so he'd gotten on board pretty quick.

She found her eyes drawn to Cameron as she stewed over how to respond to Jacob. Cameron had been trained to observe and protect, and she was always aware of where he was in a room. His blue eyes were full of respect and admiration for her. Because of Jacob's kind words or because she'd been willing to be a surrogate for Jessica? She liked that look. Pushing aside the heartache over Jessica's betrayal, she thought about going out with Cameron tonight. She'd thought they would finally go on their first date. Would he still want to date her?

"Kayt?" Jacob pulled her from staring at Cameron. "Will you accept the responsibility?"

"Yes," she said after a beat, her throat dry and scratchy.

"Thank you," Jacob breathed. "Now there are some other things Larry and I think are imperative."

"Okay?"

"Jessica knows you inside and out. She thinks she can control both of us. We've been blind to the hatred, envy, and selfishness growing in her." He sighed. "When she finds out you've taken everything from her, she's going to go after you. So we need to make sure her lawsuits won't stick."

Kaytlyn swallowed. She didn't want this. She didn't want a battle with Jessica. What would something like this do to the baby? She still could hardly wrap her mind around the baby possibly being hers. If that was true? She blew out a breath. No wonder Jessica had hardly spoken to her in the past month. "Don't give it to me. Transfer everything to someone else you trust."

"I'm sorry, Kayt. I know you. I know you don't want to be caught in the hailstorm and you'll want to protect your child, but believe me this is the best way to do that. The other problem is … there is no one else I trust completely. No one else who is genuine and has no aspirations where my money is concerned." His gaze slid to Cameron, and he smiled. "The two of you and Larry. That's it. And I'm not giving anything to that old windbag. He doesn't need or want it."

Cameron looked pleased but uncomfortable. "Thank you, sir. I'll do everything in my power to protect you."

"I know. And you'll need to protect Kayt."

The load just kept getting heavier. She still remembered those men breaking into the mansion two years ago, trying to kidnap Jacob so they could get a ransom. Luckily, their security guys had slowed them down and the police had arrived quickly. That was when they'd hired Cameron and his men. Now she would be that target. The only good part, besides the baby, was that Cameron would stay close at all times. No one would ever hurt her with him by her side.

"Happily," Cameron told Jacob. He met her gaze, and her heart leapt. Jacob was giving them his blessing to be together. The two people he trusted. She abhorred the thought that she'd lost Jessica's friendship and now she was losing Jacob, but with Cameron as her protector, she could be strong.

Her cheeks reddened. They hadn't even been on one date. Yet she thought Cameron was amazing, and obviously he and Jacob had gotten close over the past two years.

Kaytlyn beamed under his warm gaze and she thought about how there was a silver lining to everything. After two years of waiting, she would finally be able to date Cameron. Now wasn't the moment to tell Jacob the two of them were going on a date tonight, but she loved that their boss and friend seemed to already know they were interested in each other, and he had their best interests in mind. The next few weeks or months would be hard, going into a legal battle with Jessica and Peter, being pregnant, and now taking over everything. Losing Jacob would be harder, but the anticipation of growing closer to the one man she'd been undeniably drawn to would help temper those pains.

"So here's the plan," Jacob said.

The room thickened with uneasy anticipation. Jacob was brilliant and quite often had different plans to share with her, yet this one was going to change her future. She felt that as surely as she felt Cameron's gaze on her face.

CHAPTER THREE

Kaytlyn finally pulled her eyes from Cameron's handsome face and concentrated on her friend and boss's plan. Whatever it was it must be good if he thought it would protect his money from Jessica. Kaytlyn had seen enough of Jessica's explosions when she didn't get her way, and Peter was as corrupt as they came. They would both be livid when the new will came out.

Jacob started talking again, his voice stronger and more certain. "Instead of starting a fight that I might not be able to see through to the end, we're going to do all we can to make your case ironclad. We can't let Jessica and Peter have any play with an outdated will, or claiming you tricked me, or whatever they try. We'll get everything in place and blindside them after I die. They'll be behind the game and hopefully realize they can't win. Then they'll walk away. I've set up an annuity for them. At twenty grand per month, they should live comfortably, but they won't get Peter into office, at least not with my money."

Kaytlyn let him finish, then said, "So what have you and Larry schemed up?" Her mind was racing with ideas, but she had no clue how they could make her case "ironclad." Redoing the will was the only course, and Jessica and Peter could definitely challenge that. They had copies of the original will, and though she had many witnesses that could prove Jacob was in his right mind when he transferred his assets, they could definitely claim she'd tricked him into changing it before his death.

Jacob looked uncomfortable. It was an odd expression for him. Though he was physically uncomfortable most of the time, he was always in control, always confident. She found herself dreading his answer; at the same time, she leaned forward to make sure she heard him clearly.

"Well, my dear," he said, "this is where the second gutsy question comes from me to you. Do you want to protect our legacy and make sure Peter can't get his hands on it?"

"Yes." Despite the sick sorrow she felt over Jessica's duplicity and betrayal, she also felt an odd sort of relief. The signs of her being unstable and deluded by Peter were all there. At least they'd found out the truth before he passed and all of that money and Jacob's businesses went to support Peter. Worse, her foundation was destroyed to support them. She wasn't trying to excuse Jessica, but she blamed Peter for deluding and twisting her former friend. Yet what about the baby? Possibly her child. She focused on what she could control right now. "We can't let them destroy your life's work, or my foundation." Kaytlyn's resolve grew as she thought everything through.

"I thought you'd say that." His face was grim and determined. "Now what I'm about to ask of you can't leave this room."

Kaytlyn exchanged a glance with Cameron. They both nodded.

"Larry and I have been up most of the night, and we agree that what I'm about to ask of you is unconventional, but it should be our strongest play. You need to realize also that your biggest battle will come after I pass. Blindsided, Jessica and Peter will be scrambling hard to fight, but everything will already be in place."

Kaytlyn hated the thought of Jacob passing. She would be lonely and overwhelmed without his counsel on business matters every day. Yet now the businesses would be hers. She didn't want them for the financial gain, but she'd been overseeing most things since Jacob had been diagnosed, and she'd protect them from Peter's schemes. Maybe someday she could admit they were Jessica's schemes too, but she was still wrapping her mind around it all.

Jacob took a long breath, and Kaytlyn wondered why he was so reluctant to ask her whatever he and Larry had decided upon.

"It's okay," Kaytlyn reassured him. "I'll do whatever we need to do. We're a team. You and I. Always."

He squeezed her hand. "I love you, Kayt. You're the most incredible person I've ever known. I love my daughter, as I know you do as well. I always will love Jessica, but now that I know the truth, I realize I should've seen the signs and not been so shocked by her betrayal. You have no deceitfulness in you at all. You're loyal, grateful, and angelic all the way through."

Jacob had never before been so complimentary or told her he

loved her. She loved him like an uncle, definitely like a best friend. He'd done so much for her—teaching and inspiring and lifting. She'd do anything for him. "I love you too, Jacob," she said simply.

His gaze flickered to Cameron. "Son. I know I can trust you, and that's why you're here. Kaytlyn is more priceless than any asset she will now own. You guard her with your life."

Cameron replied with a solemn nod.

"This goes beyond money," Jacob said sternly. "I've spoken with Sutton and have his approval. With your consent, I'm putting ten million dollars in your account and hiring you away from Sutton, with the sole purpose of you staying by Kaytlyn's side day and night."

Cameron sat even straighter. "For how long, sir?"

"As long as she needs you."

"Jacob," Kaytlyn protested. Heat traced through her at the thought of being so close to this attractive man, but she didn't think this was acceptable. "Do you understand what you're asking? He never gets a day off? Any kind of break?" She had been excited twenty minutes ago about the prospect of dating Cameron and being protected by him, but she couldn't take away the man's foreseeable future.

"I understand exactly what I'm asking, and I think Cameron does as well." He arched an eyebrow at Cameron.

"I do, sir."

"What's your answer?"

Cameron gazed deeply into Kaytlyn's eyes, as if she was the queen and he was the knight pledging his loyalty and life to her. That was nuts. They weren't living in medieval times. His eyes were tender and deep, and she couldn't look away—especially when he said, "My answer is yes."

Kaytlyn's own eyes widened and her stomach pitched. "Yes? You're committing to protect me? Solely focus on me?"

Cameron nodded. No indecision. No fear. He was fully committed to ... her.

Excitement stirred in her breast, mingling with a sense of safety and comfort. Yet a sense of dread crept in too. If Cameron was her protector, could he date her? After Jacob told them whatever proposal he had and they got everything settled with him, she and Cameron would have to figure out if going on an innocent date was still in the equation. She certainly hoped so, but there were so many heavy things weighing on her mind, and wonderful things growing within her. Would Cameron want to date a single mother? Was she truly this little one's mother?

"Now for the idea Larry and I believe will secure your future and protect my fortune." Jacob's smile was strained. She was beginning to wonder how much longer he'd draw the suspense out when he rushed ahead: "Kayt, I need you to marry me and have my child."

Kaytlyn sputtered and yanked back away from him. "What?" She was already expecting. What was he saying?

Cameron stood, towering over both of them. "You just hired me to protect her, and I'll protect her from you if I need to."

Jacob held up his hands. "Calm down, both of you. The marriage will be in name only." He dipped his head toward Kaytlyn. "If Peter could unethically use your egg, and they both know we can prove that by in utero testing, I don't think they're going to want an ugly legal battle if we claim the baby is mine."

Cameron didn't sit back down. His gaze swiveled from Jacob to Kaytlyn, his blue eyes stormy and unsettled.

Kaytlyn's mind was whirling. Marry Jacob? Her first thought was that she couldn't possibly be intimate with her best friend, but he'd said the marriage would be in name only, so that made her stomach a little less nauseated. She hadn't had morning sickness yet, but she imagined it would feel like this. The second thought was that Jacob was trying to protect her and her baby. He'd claim the child for the world to see, and she wouldn't have to share a child with Peter. Her third thought was that she definitely wouldn't be able to date Cameron if she agreed, but how could she possibly refuse Jacob, the man who had given her everything?

"Sit down," Jacob said to Cameron.

"I'd prefer standing."

Jacob focused on Kaytlyn. "I wouldn't ask this of you if I didn't feel strongly that it's the only way to ensure my legacy stays safe from Jessica and Peter. We'd be married in a private ceremony tonight, and your baby will be my heir."

Marry Jacob? It was insane, and yet it might be the solution. She knew that Peter, and possibly Jessica, would stop at nothing to get Jacob's money, ruin everything Kaytlyn and Jacob had worked so hard for, and get into political office, using the fortune to push him all the way to the top. If Kaytlyn agreed to this plan, she could at least slow down their evil schemes, and her baby— her legitimate baby—would have a father who Kaytlyn thought the world of instead of the scum who really was her child's father.

Jacob's gaze begged her to agree. She knew he wasn't doing any of this for himself; he was doing it for her and for all the people they employed, all the small towns that relied on their jobs for their lifeblood. Even more importantly, her foundation would continue to protect and help children throughout the world. So many factors played into it, and if Peter and Jessica won ... Kaytlyn shuddered thinking of all that money, billions of dollars, being used to hurt and destroy.

She wanted to look at Cameron and get his opinion. Her new round-the-clock protection. Who knew what that was going to look like? Yet if she agreed, she would be married. Married in name only, but it still meant no more flirting with or going on dates with Cameron.

"Please, Kayt. You know this isn't for me. I've gone round and round it in my mind and with Larry. Even though I'm gifting you everything right now, they could try and fight it, but if you're my wife and have my child, the new will should protect everything. Peter won't want it coming out that he used your egg without your permission. It's the right path," Jacob said, as decisive and in control as he always was.

Kaytlyn feared he was probably right, and she trusted Jacob more than she'd ever trusted anyone. For ten years he'd been training her and worked with her. He would never ask anything that wasn't in her best interest. She knew it as surely as she knew her eyes were blue.

She could feel Cameron's angst simmering next to her, but he didn't say anything.

She looked into Jacob's eyes, weary from the battle with cancer but still alight with intelligence and goodness. He'd spent his entire life working and accumulating funds so he could help others, and now it was her turn to take the cause forward. They both knew he wasn't long for this world. Over three months ago, the doctors had given him weeks to live. Only his sheer determination and grit were keeping him alive. She'd be lost without him. If she agreed, she'd soon be a billionaire, a widow, and a single mother. She'd thought she was being a surrogate for Jessica and Peter. Everything had been flipped in the past half hour.

"I'll do it," she heard herself say. Her voice sounded like it was coming through a tunnel, and the entire moment felt surreal. She heard Cameron suck in a breath.

Jacob nodded. "You're going to do amazing things, Kaytlyn. I trust you to raise our child to be exactly as good as you are."

Our child. How she appreciated him assuming a responsibility that hadn't been either of theirs, and making her feel so much less alone in the world. Kaytlyn felt tears stinging her eyes. This was crazy, but it felt right too, which maybe made it crazier. She gave Jacob a watery smile and then let herself look at Cameron. He was still standing, arms folded across his chest, brows knit together with concern. This man would protect her, but sadly they couldn't be anything more.

The situation reminded her of King Arthur, Lady Guinevere, and Sir Lancelot, but this was no legend and their battle was against two of the most underhanded people Kaytlyn knew. She'd always suspected as much of Peter, but to know Jessica now hated her and was motivated only by money and power hurt deeply.

Her eyes traveled over Cameron's strong form. He could easily protect her physically, but this fight was going to be emotional, sneaky, and dirty, and it would be fought in the courts.

Her life had changed four weeks ago when she'd become pregnant with her friend's baby, well former friend. This was another life-changing moment, and a lot of responsibility, but she felt equal to the task. She prayed she could truly do amazing things and raise her child to be even better than she and Jacob could imagine. Her child. So exciting and scary. The vision she saw right now showed her doing it alone, but at least the child would have a father and a legacy to fulfill.

Cameron's large frame overshadowed her and brought some comfort and reassurance. She had a protector and an ally, but that was all he could be, and from the look in his eyes, he knew it as well as she did.

CHAPTER FOUR

Cameron Bodily paced next to Jacob Tarbet's bedside. Twenty minutes ago, Cameron had been handed a gift he'd been craving for two years: a date with the angelically beautiful, smart, witty, loyal, kind ... He could list complimentary adjectives for Kaytlyn Klein all day long. He'd been falling for her and working up the nerve to ask her out. She was his boss every bit as much as Jacob was, and he didn't want to step over any lines. She'd taken that worry out of the equation, teasing with him and agreeing to go out tonight.

Then they'd walked into Jacob's room, and such innocence as a date with his perfect woman was shattered. Jacob had asked Kaytlyn to wait in the office at the bottom of the stairs for Cameron. She'd have plenty of work to do, as she always did, and she was safe with the staff and security all in place at the high-functioning thirty-thousand-square-foot mansion, nestled at the base of the mountain in Sun Valley, Idaho.

Jacob let Cameron pace, not saying anything. Obviously, Jacob knew how upset Cameron was and how much he disagreed with this course of action. *Disagreed* wasn't a strong enough word. Jacob was right that this might be the only way to protect his charity, businesses, properties, and money from his scheming daughter and son-in-law, but it wasn't fair to expect this of Kaytlyn. Too much had already been asked of her. She was carrying Peter and Jessica's baby? Possibly her own baby? His emotions were all over the place. If he saw Peter he might tear the man apart with his bare hands.

"How could you?" Cameron blurted as he rounded on the man he respected as much as he did his own father, his military brothers, and Sutton Smith. "How could you ask it of her?"

Jacob splayed his hands; his dark eyes were somber. "I've been praying and stewing about this most of the night, son. I was so low. I mean, I've seen how crafty, explosive, and selfish Jessica could be, worried about it throughout the years—especially when she married Peter, who's obviously a politician and would lie to his own mother. But to hear it from her own lips, that she would destroy everything, destroy Kaytlyn, that she hated Kaytlyn. Kaytlyn who's done so much for her, was willing to carry her child." He shook his head. "I still can't believe all the things she said. She was obviously out of control, but it was almost as if she really wanted me to hear them, had wanted to say them to me and Kaytlyn for years.

"It's been awful to have to admit to myself ..." His voice dropped. "That I've failed and my daughter is a monster. It wasn't enough to just change the will. I can't risk any of it falling into Peter's hands. I'm not trying to excuse my daughter but he's changed her, and not for the better. Kaytlyn has to be married to me, and I have to claim her baby is mine to protect the child from Peter. But I'm doing all of this for her and for the people she helps, protects, and lifts. Do you think I came by this plan easily?"

Cameron pressed his lips together, and his jaw hurt from clenching it. "No. I know how deliberate and conscientious you are, but Kaytlyn ..." Cameron had thought he'd never love again when he'd lost his college girlfriend in a car rollover ten years ago. Maybe he shouldn't even think the word *love* with Kaytlyn —more respect, desire, friendship—yet he could let his mind go to love, and it did. He held himself in check around her only because of years of military training.

"I believe Jessica was telling the truth about the baby," Jacob said, interrupting his thoughts. "That it's really Kaytlyn's." He shook his head. "I wanted to advise Kaytlyn against being their surrogate but how could I do that to my own daughter? Peter is such a snake and I've seen the way he leers at Kaytlyn. It made me mad for Jessica's sake. Especially now I know the man has cheated on Jessica multiple times. I think the man got his sick wish of having Kaytlyn be the mother of his child."

"I'll kill him," Cameron seethed, and he meant it.

"You might get the chance." Jacob studied him. "This is going to be a rough path, fighting Peter and Jessica. Kaytlyn's going to need you, but she's strong ... unbelievably strong."

Cameron knew how strong she was, but he hoped that she might truly need him. He'd be there for her, any way he could.

"I know," Jacob commiserated. "I hate what she's going through with Jessica's betrayal and Peter's manipulation. She's a special angel, isn't she?"

Cameron nodded shortly. That was one way of phrasing it. She was perfect to him, and Peter had taken advantage of her kindness. Somehow Cameron would make the man pay.

"You do realize Protect the Young is Kaytlyn's brainchild and she's done most of the work?"

Another nod. Cameron knew how smart and charitably minded she was, having observed her and Jacob far too closely the past two years as they worked, dreamed, and implemented together. He knew their relationship was platonic, but he'd been jealous of that closeness. If he was honest, the main thing bugging him right now was that he wanted Kaytlyn for himself.

"And you realize Peter could destroy all of that? Pull the funding from the children and mothers who need it so badly?"

Cameron pushed out a heavy breath and sank into the chair next to Jacob's bed. "But marrying Kaytlyn and you pretending the baby is yours? You believe this idea is bulletproof? That Peter and Jessica can't come after her?" Kaytlyn would have a huge target on her back, and not just for being a gorgeous billionaire. Cameron wouldn't put it past Jessica and Peter to try to take her out. They'd struck him as two-faced almost every time he'd been around them. He felt bad that Jacob had to face the truth, but at the same time, it was good it had been uncovered.

"Legally, I think we'll be covered, but it hit me early this morning. I'm afraid Peter, and Jessica, can stoop pretty low. I don't want anyone to hurt Kaytlyn." He winced as he said it, and Cameron understood how sickening it was to think of Kaytlyn being hurt. He also had a brief insight into the betrayal Jacob was going through, with his child going against everything he believed in and had worked so hard for. "That's why I've hired you to never leave Kaytlyn's side."

Cameron passed a hand over his face. "You do realize how hard it will be for me to be close to her but ... not?"

Jacob stared deeply into his eyes. "I've noticed. Of course I have. You know how deep her beauty is, how impressive she is. You want her to be yours more than you've ever wanted anything in this world."

Cameron's eyes widened. He thought he'd behaved above reproach regarding Kaytlyn. "How did you get all of that from a few wayward glances?"

Jacob smirked. "I'm dying, but I'm not dead yet."

"We set up a date for tonight, before ..."

"I'm sorry, son. I've messed up your plans. You're going to have to put them on hold." Jacob cleared his throat, shifted on the bed, and said, "Do you trust me?"

Cameron's back straightened. "Yes, sir."

"How much?"

"As much as any person I know." There was no deception or guile with Jacob. He was the best person Cameron had ever been around, besides Kaytlyn. That was partly why this idea was so shocking and hard to wrap his mind around. The Jacob he knew and respected would never ask for anything selfish or unethical.

Not that this marriage was unethical, but if they didn't consummate it, thank heavens, was it really a marriage?

"Please trust that this is for Kaytlyn. To protect her baby and her foundation. Also to try to keep Peter out of office. This scheme isn't an old man wanting to parade around a hot young wife, or me fulfilling some fantasies by being married to the most amazing woman I know."

Cameron met his gaze evenly. Jacob was taking Kaytlyn's baby as his own. It was a noble move, one Cameron honestly wished he could do, but he knew his role. He was the soldier. "I believe you."

Jacob sighed. "And if you trust me, I need you to promise me something."

Cameron had already promised to protect Kaytlyn night and day. If only that meant he could truly be with her ... but with her married to Jacob, he'd have to bury his desire for her deep. Even if it was only a marriage in name, it was still a marriage. "Anything, sir." No matter how upset he was with what was happening and had happened to Kaytlyn, he would be loyal to her and Jacob.

"Keep yourself in control, son. Don't act on the desire and love you have for Kaytlyn."

"Of course I will stay in control." He was offended at the suggestion. "You'll be married to her, sir."

Jacob looked at him with a wizened glance. "We both know I'm not long for this world. When I pass, you'll still need to stay strong."

Cameron froze. He blinked a couple of times and said, "I'm not going to be waiting around for you to die so I can pursue her, sir."

"I wouldn't blame you if you did. But she's going to need some time and lots of patience. Jessica's betrayal has already changed her. The baby will change her as well, especially if it's truly hers. I hired you to be with her night and day for more than just physical protection. I feel you're the man that can be there for her, but you have to take it slow. Let it be on her terms. Put her needs before your own."

Cameron understood what Jacob was saying. If he cared for Kaytlyn, he'd need to be in this for the long haul. He nodded decisively and extended his hand.

Jacob shook it—not with the strength he'd used two years ago when Cameron was first hired on to protect the man, but there was still firmness in the grip. "You're a great man, Cameron Bodily. I'm trusting you with so much. Thank you for being worthy of that trust."

Cameron's throat tightened. He wanted to be the man Jacob thought he was, the man his mother and father had always inspired him to be. "Thank you, sir."

Tiredly, Jacob released his hand and waved toward the door. "Go, keep Kayt safe."

Once Cameron had closed the door behind him, he leaned against it and closed his eyes in a brief prayer. *Help me be strong, Lord. In so many ways.* He'd always been strong physically, but emotionally he'd broken when Lori had died. He didn't want to go back there, ever. Yet he felt like Kaytlyn meant more to him already than anyone ever had, and the angelic woman was dealing with so much.

"Cameron?" Kaytlyn's soft voice and her smooth fingers on his arm jerked him away from the door and out of any thoughts of prayer.

He stared down at her. Jacob was right: she did have the face of an angel. She was perfectly beautiful with fine-boned features, smooth skin, beguiling blue eyes, and the most perfect rosebud lips. There was such sweetness and kindness in her countenance. How had Peter and Jessica taken advantage of her like this? His promise to Jacob swirled around them. Cameron would protect her, even if that meant protecting her from himself.

"Are you okay?" she asked sweetly.

"Am I okay?" Cameron pushed out a groan. "I'm not the one anyone is concerned about at the moment."

She smiled. "I'm concerned. You've given up the foreseeable future ... to protect me."

"It's worth it," he said swiftly and maybe too forcefully.

Her entire countenance was so full of trust and love, he found his hand lifting toward her face. He wanted to just touch the smooth cheek, have her lean into his palm. Those beautiful eyes filled with trust and love for him. Was he seeing this right? She'd been through something horrible and was now agreeing to take on the responsibility of Jacob's businesses, in addition to her future child, and do it all while fighting Jessica and Peter. This woman was incredible, and she seemed to care for him as much as he did for her.

His hand cupped her cheek, and she softly leaned into him. His voice felt gravelly as he forced out the words. "I'm sorry about all of this." He tilted his head toward her abdomen. "Peter and Jessica tricking you."

Kaytlyn straightened away from his hand. He didn't blame her, but oh, how he wished he could comfort her and take her pain away. She put her hands protectively over her abdomen. "I'm going to protect my baby."

Cameron's admiration for her shot through the roof. "And I'm going to protect you."

Kaytlyn bit at her lip but gave him a grateful nod.

"I will *never* let anyone hurt you or your baby."

She studied him for a few beats and then nodded. "I believe you."

Cameron had sworn to protect her for as long as she needed. He'd never felt any pledge more deeply.

"I guess this means no date tonight," she said softly.

"I guess you're right." He wondered if a time would come when he could date her. Not now, not with all she was dealing with.

"This is going to be hard for you," she guessed.

"You have no idea." Cameron shook his head, disgusted with himself. That was nothing he should be admitting to. She was all that mattered, not his desire to be there for her in every way or how much he cared for her. His focus was on helping and protecting her. His spine straightened, and he knew this job would take as much strength as any job he'd had in the military. "I'll be fine," he said. "All that matters is protecting you."

She stared at him as if trying to see past his military veneer into his heart. Maybe someday he could allow that. Not today. Not in the foreseeable future. He'd give up anything to be close to her, to protect her, but he would honor her marriage to Jacob and he would honor the instruction Jacob had given. Even after their friend and boss passed, Cameron would be strong until the time was right. He sure hoped Jacob would come back as an angel and inform him when that time was, because as much as Cameron wanted to be close to Kaytlyn, he feared Jacob wouldn't even be cold in the ground before he made a play for her heart. That was horrible to even think, so he forced it away.

Kaytlyn finally stepped back, and a professional shutter went over her blue gaze. She was sweetness personified, but she could be tough when she needed to be. "I'll be in my office."

She spun on her heel and walked away. Cameron followed.

They got down the grand staircase and went across the foyer toward the large office off the entryway. The windows stretched from floor to third-story ceiling, and they were framed with wood timbers in the foyer. Though the four-story mansion was sprawling and massive, it had a warm, cozy feel with all the wood and a distinctive Sun Valley flair.

Kaytlyn whirled on him, placing a hand on her hip and tossing her long blond hair. "Does guarding me night and day mean you're my shadow now?"

Cameron let a small smile escape. "Yes, ma'am, it does." Dang, this was going to be tough. She was just too cute and appealing.

"Well, you're going to be very bored as I sit in my office hour after hour."

"I've dealt with boredom before." He'd been in the military. She had no clue how often he'd had to sit and watch and wait in situations much more uncomfortable than this one.

"Fine." She sashayed into the office.

Cameron watched her go, then scrubbed at his eyes with his fists. If he was supposed to watch Kaytlyn night and day and then not act on the desire inside of him, maybe his boss could've poked his eyes out first to make it easier on him.

CHAPTER FIVE

The next two weeks went by in a blur for Kaytlyn. She worked long hours getting everything in place with their businesses and especially her foundation, as she wanted focus on her future baby and spend time with her husband before he passed. Just as Jacob had said, they were married that night with his friend Larry as the clergy—he was a leader in his local church —and Cameron as the witness. Cameron's jaw had been so tight, it looked like it was carved from granite. Kaytlyn tried to avoid looking at him throughout the short ceremony, but she could feel his eyes burning her from behind.

In some ways, nothing had changed, yet everything felt new. Cameron was less than ten feet away everywhere she went, and her baby was growing within her. Her baby. She wanted to dance, laugh, and cry all at the same time when she thought about it.

She had gone to the doctor, done a test to determine if the baby was truly hers, and heard the baby's heartbeat. Miraculous. She should hate Peter and Jessica for tricking her, but she felt like she'd been given a gift, no matter who the father was. She could honestly say she was more excited about her baby than anything she'd ever anticipated, and she often found herself touching her abdomen or imagining what the baby would look like. Hopefully nothing like Peter.

She wasn't quite as excited about her current circumstances. Cameron's constant presence was driving her crazy. They used to have a comfortable relationship, some teasing and flirtations, and a lot of significant glances. Now he'd become a statue, shadowing her but rarely speaking to her or showing any emotion at all. She missed the old Cameron, but she didn't know what she expected. She was married, pregnant, and would soon be the recipient of billions of dollars in businesses and properties. Of course things would change between them.

The first six weeks of her pregnancy hadn't been physically taxing, though emotionally she was overwrought. She worked long hours at their home office, conducting numerous video chats with their managers. Her and Jacob trusted their managers and had great people in place, but she wanted to make sure everything was ready so she could take time off when she had the baby. Jacob grew frailer every day as she visited him morning and evening, but he constantly expressed how grateful he was for her, even though they were both still sick about Jessica's duplicity. They still were able to hash out business ideas and problems, and though he was already months past the doctor's prediction of his mortality, she didn't feel like he would leave her any time soon.

The middle of July grew warmer and even more beautiful in their little valley. She'd cut back on lifting weights, and she missed the times when she and Cameron used to run into each other in the mansion's nicely furnished basement weight room. Cameron must be waking early to fit his own workouts in, because he shadowed her whenever she was awake. He'd moved his things into the suite next to hers and she swore he had a beeper on her, though she couldn't find it.

Often in the afternoon or evenings, she'd go on hikes up the mountain trails, and of course Cameron would come. She loved being out in nature and Cameron's presence offered stability, safety, and an excitement she couldn't dismiss. Sometimes on their walks, Cameron would relax enough to talk with her; they'd share childhood stories, or he'd give her some insight into military life, or she'd tell him about a touching email she'd received from their charitable work or some new idea she had to help a group or person.

She didn't feel like she was in any danger. Jessica had called Jacob a few times, acting as if she hadn't had her breakdown fit, but she hadn't so much as texted Kaytlyn. It shouldn't still hurt but Kaytlyn had once believed they were close friends. When Jessica found out about the change in the will, the marriage, and that Kaytlyn was going to fight for her baby, she would go nuts.

Kaytlyn woke up toward the end of July with her stomach churning. She couldn't swallow down the nastiness in her mouth, and she was afraid to move. The doctor had warned her that morning sickness might be coming soon, and she'd felt a little bit of queasiness in the past few days, but she hadn't realized it could hit so strongly. She groaned, rolled onto her side, and tried not to move further, afraid she'd vomit.

Her phone started ringing, and she ignored it. Even the slight movement of answering it might be too much. She drifted back off to sleep but awoke to a tap on the door. She stared blearily at it, hoping the person would go away and leave her to her misery.

"Kaytlyn?" Cameron called through the door.

She knew she should respond, but if she did, she might lose whatever was in her stomach.

"Kayt?" His voice grew more concerned, and she couldn't help but notice that he'd used her nickname. He'd never done that before. He turned the doorknob and swung the door open. His eyes landed on her curled in the bed, and then they widened. "I'm sorry. Do you want me to leave, or do you need help?"

She swallowed hard and shook her head slightly; the tiny movement made her stomach pitch. She didn't want him to see her like this, but she couldn't remember the last time she had felt this miserable. How long was morning sickness supposed to last, and who was going to deal with all the work she had laid out for today if she didn't get her rear out of bed?

He approached the bed slowly, apprehensively. Kaytlyn wanted to reassure him that she would be okay, but she was afraid to open her mouth for fear of vomiting all over him. The little one growing within her had felt like a thrilling, mystical, far-off dream; now it was the source of a nauseating nightmare.

Cameron stopped a couple feet shy of the bed. "Jacob's really concerned about you. He said he's called and you're not answering, and you've never slept in this late before. Is it the baby?"

"Morning sickness," she managed to get out. "Baby's fine." She remembered the doctor saying that morning sickness was a good sign that the pregnancy was going well. Right now, she couldn't say she agreed.

Cameron eased closer and squatted down next to the bed so he was eye level with her, and much too close for the awful state she was in. Even in her misery, Kaytlyn was humiliated that he was seeing her like this, but it was nothing compared to the fear of spewing chunks all over him. She imagined she looked and even smelled disgusting.

"But *you're* not fine," he said softly. "What can I do for you?"

She loved seeing him so concerned for her, but she couldn't dwell on all the things she loved about him. Nervous sweat beaded on her brow as she swallowed down the nasty taste in her mouth again.

Forcing a smile she didn't feel, she managed to say, "I don't know." She spent so much time working and researching the best spot for a new women's shelter or orphanage, how to get supplies to an area after a disaster, and teaching teenage girls and young moms how to improve their skills and become more marketable for a job, yet she hadn't stopped and researched what she might need on hand if she got morning sicknesses. If the doctor had given suggestions for feeling better at her last appointment, she couldn't remember them.

"I'll go talk to Cathy and research it," Cameron said decisively. "You'll be okay for a few minutes?"

"Yep," she mumbled.

He smiled and reached out a hand, as if he would smooth the

hair away from her face or something. Kaytlyn literally ached to feel his touch, and she felt herself arching toward him.

Cameron froze, and his concern for her turned to a look of almost horror. His hand dropped away, and he straightened and marched from the room.

Kaytlyn watched him go. He was so strong, attractive, and perfect, and she wished their situation could be different. She usually kept herself busy enough to shove the feelings for him to the back burner. Lying here miserable and wanting to concentrate on anything but the unsettled feeling in her stomach, she couldn't stop the memories of him smiling at her, saying something funny, and doing something thoughtful for her or Jacob.

Jacob. As she thought about her friend, her worries about Cameron fell into perspective. She'd done this to herself, married Jacob of her own free will to protect her child, his businesses, and their foundation. It didn't matter that it wasn't a real marriage; she was committed to it now for reasons so much bigger than her selfish desires. She could not allow her mind to wander toward Cameron.

She hadn't moved when Cameron appeared at the door, with a food tray in his hand and a triumphant smile on his face. Unfortunately, the latter made him even more handsome. "Did you know Cathy is a mother of nine and grandmother of twenty-five?" he asked.

Kaytlyn tried to nod.

"Of course you did. You're more thoughtful than the rest of us."

Kaytlyn appreciated the compliment, but she didn't dare voice her gratitude.

Cameron set the tray on the bedside table. "So we need to get some crackers or a few bites of toast in you and this ginger tea. Can you sit up?"

She really didn't think so, and even the smell of toast turned her stomach. *Please don't vomit.* "Maybe."

He came close enough for Kaytlyn to catch a whiff of his clean, crisp scent. Why didn't it turn her stomach like the toast did? His brow furrowed as if he wasn't sure how to help her. He reached out, then drew back, then reached out again. Kaytlyn would've found it comical if she weren't so miserable.

Finally, with his face settling into determination, he slid one hand underneath her while putting his other hand on her bare arm. He gently lifted her up and then settled her against the headboard. His hands on her skin felt so good that she was almost able to put her revolting stomach out of mind, but the slight movement to sitting wasn't good for her nausea. She took slow breaths, praying she wouldn't lose it as Cameron carefully lifted her forward to position pillows behind her back.

Straightening, he watched her for a few seconds, then asked, "Better?"

Kaytlyn was surprised to find that sitting up was a little better now. She relaxed into the pillows and nodded. "Thank you."

"My pleasure."

The way he said those words sent awareness coursing through her, especially when his cheeks darkened and he looked away quickly. He'd acted so stoic around her since she'd married Jacob. Not that she blamed him, but sometimes she wondered if the pull between them was one-sided now. If he was so strong that he could simply shut off his feelings, maybe he wouldn't want to date her when she was able to. That day seemed too far in the future. She had a legacy to protect and a baby to raise.

"Toast?" he asked brightly, lifting a piece off the tray.

Kaytlyn nodded and reached out for the toast, but he brought it right to her lips. She nibbled at it, chewed, and swallowed. When that didn't make her vomit, she tried a little more. Cameron watched her steadily as he held the toast for her. When she'd eaten several bites and her stomach felt a little more settled, she murmured, "Thank you."

He set the toast down and brought the teacup to her lips. She sipped some of the fragrant ginger tea. She couldn't force her eyes away from his handsome face, as it was so sweet that this tough, larger-than-life man was feeding her. She'd been on her own for over ten years and couldn't remember the last time someone took care of her. She and Jacob were great partners and friends, but even though he'd treated her almost like a daughter he'd never ministered to her like this.

She waved the tea off; her stomach felt remarkably better.

"Better?" he asked, setting it down on the tray.

"Yes. Thank you so much."

"It's what I'm here for."

She smiled. "I thought you were the tough military man who was here to knock heads through the wall if they got out of line."

He chuckled. "That's my favorite role, but feeding toast to beautiful ladies is right up there too." His face blanched as he realized that he'd complimented her. He'd been so careful since she'd married Jacob and she admired him for it, but she didn't care if he slipped up.

"I can't possibly look beautiful right now," she said.

His eyes swept over her and he said quietly. "You always look beautiful." He backed away. "I'll just ... go tell Jacob you're all right. I'll be back to check on you soon."

"Thanks." Kaytlyn watched him go. He gave her one more smile as he softly shut the door.

It wasn't easy being married to a dying man twice her age to prevent his fortune from falling into his sadistic son-in-law's hands. Yet Kaytlyn couldn't imagine anything as miserable as how much she ached to be near Cameron Bodily and how she couldn't let herself dream of him.

Cameron hurried from Kaytlyn's suite. Being so close to her was torture. Even when she was sick and disheveled, she was so appealing that it about killed him to look at her and not declare his undying devotion. When he'd touched her smooth skin to reposition her in the bed and her silky hair had brushed his arm while her sweet vanilla scent had washed over him, he'd about lost it and pulled her close.

She is married, she is married, he repeated over and over in his head. Usually it cooled his ardor, but usually he didn't let himself get close enough to touch or smell her. Even though he was her protection and went everywhere with her, he was able to stay back and keep his emotions in check. Feeding her like that was too much.

He hurried through the wide halls and rapped on Jacob's door, heard a muffled "Come in," and swung it wide. He strode to his friend and boss's bedside. He and Jacob had grown even closer lately.

"How is she?" Jacob asked.

Cameron shook his head. "She's really sick."

Jacob cursed softly.

"My thoughts exactly," Cameron muttered.

Jacob stared up at him. His cheeks were gaunt, and his eyes were sunken. "I'm holding on as long as I can ..." He drew a few steadying breaths, then continued, "But I'm afraid you're going to be on your own soon."

Cameron sank into the chair next to the bed. He couldn't stand the thought of Jacob dying. He had a question he had to ask, though. "You still feel we need to wait to inform Jessica and Peter about the transfer of your business and assets, the new will, your marriage, and Kaytlyn's claim on the baby?"

Jacob nodded.

"But what if ..." Cameron hated to say it.

"I don't want to give them any extra time to assemble their case."

"I just hate to have her face them alone." He studied his hands as he twisted them.

Jacob placed a hand over his. "She won't be alone. She has you."

Cameron stared steadily into Jacob's blue eyes; they were still clear, despite the pain on his face. It broke Cameron's heart that Jacob and Kaytlyn, once such powerful friends and business partners, were now married yet living on opposite sides of the mansion, sick and miserable, with him as the liaison. His role here was tough and sometimes weird.

"Are you still my man, Cameron?"

"Always, sir." Those words might sound cheesy, but Cameron felt them deeply and he knew the older man did as well.

"Thank you. Go watch over Kayt, please. Tell her I'm praying she'll feel better soon."

"Okay." Cameron stood and strode from the room. *Watch over Kayt.* The job should've been easy, as there was no immediate danger, but it was the hardest job he'd ever had in his life. He had to fight to stay detached from the incredible woman he was assigned to. He'd take fighting terrorists in Kuwait over being so close to his dream woman and yet so far away.

CHAPTER SIX

Six more weeks passed in a horrid blur. Kaytlyn spent more time leaning over the toilet than she did with her computer or on her phone. The only constant and bright light throughout the wretched time was Cameron. He and the head housekeeper, Cathy, spoiled her and watched over her. At first, Kaytlyn was humiliated to have Cameron see her sick, but he never treated her with anything but kindness and almost reverence. He was still very careful to touch her as little as possible, and he tried not to say anything that would lead her to think about him intimately, but he was her rock: feeding her, bringing her anything she needed, even helping her tap out emails and conduct video chats on her computer by her bedside. She soon learned he was as capable with business as he was with security.

It was late August, and Kaytlyn was having one of the worst days she could remember. Peering out the view of her picture windows, she hated that she'd lost most of this gorgeous summer to lying in her bed. Immediately, she felt guilty for the selfish thought. Jacob had been withering away for almost a year and never complained. Cameron was healthy and could've been hiking, biking, or swimming—he'd even shared that he loved water skiing on the nearby Redfish Lake—yet he chose to spend his time in her suite, missing out on the warmth and sunshine.

She needed to get up, shower, and do something with this day, but despite the usual crackers, toast, and ginger tea that Cameron brought her every morning, her stomach wasn't settling today. She was almost twelve weeks along and the morning sickness was supposed to stop. Not for her, apparently.

A soft rap on the door announced that Cameron was back from checking on Jacob.

"Come in," she forced out.

He strode into the room, looking as strong and handsome as ever in a soft grey T-shirt and black pants. His face softened as he looked at her. She admired him for not making advances on her since she'd been married, but she loved that she could still see deep in his eyes how much he cared. It was more of an emotional attachment now, born of her gratitude for his patient nursing, but she could admit to herself that she was desperately in love with him.

His blue eyes were even more concerned than normal. "Kayt," he said softly. "I've got to get you to Jacob's room."

Something in his voice terrified her. She sat up too quickly and almost lost her toast. Cameron rushed toward her bed, but he stopped before reaching out to her. She swallowed several times, then croaked, "What's wrong?"

"He's so frail today, and he and I both are afraid he doesn't have too much longer."

No! Was Jacob going to leave her today? He'd outlived every doctor's prophecy, but she wasn't ready to be pregnant and alone, managing more businesses than any person she'd met—not to mention her foundation—and dealing with the wrath she knew would come from Peter and Jessica. Cameron stood by the side of her bed, and she glanced up and met his gaze. At least she had him.

"Do you want to ... take a shower, and then we'll go?"

"Do I smell that bad?" she tossed back at him.

He smiled, much to her relief. "No. I just thought you might feel better."

She would. Throwing back the covers, she forced her legs underneath her. Her stomach was tumbling, but she tried with everything in her to ignore it. Cameron was right there. He didn't touch her, but she could smell his clean scent and she could never forget how amazing and thoughtful he was. Who would've guessed the tough military man could care for a sickly pregnant woman with such tenderness and patience?

They made it to the bathroom, and he thoughtfully started the shower. She leaned against the glass shower door, the cool glass soothing to her cheek.

"I'll just ... wait outside," he muttered.

"Good plan."

Cameron's eyebrows jumped and he quickly strode from the room, shutting the door behind him.

Kaytlyn laughed at how uncomfortable he'd been. The only other choice was to cry at what a hot mess she was: in love with her protector while pregnant and in a fake marriage with her boss and friend. Could life get any worse?

She peeled off her clothes and studied her reflection in the mirror. She wished she had at least a baby bump, but she supposed she'd lost too much weight not being able to hold down food. She used to have a nice shape, she thought, but the woman staring back at her looked scrawny and malnourished. Great. She was not only sickly and disgusting; now she looked like a skeleton.

She stepped into the shower, laughing at her messed-up life, and promptly threw up all over the shower. Yes, life could definitely not get any worse.

Cameron paced outside Kaytlyn's suite, sweat popping up on his brow at the thought of her in the shower. *Don't go there. Please don't go there.* Any romantic thoughts of her made his job of staying detached a hundred times harder, as if just being around the sweet, tough, and brilliant Kaytlyn wasn't hard enough. He was amazed that she could patiently deal with an unplanned pregnancy, the sickness, the workload, and the worries over Jacob.

He clenched his fists and thought about Jacob wasting away in that bed. That helped him redirect. He had an awful feeling that Jacob was just holding on until he said goodbye to Kaytlyn. He'd never seen someone look so close to death as Jacob had looked this morning. He'd seen plenty of people he cared about already dead: Lori, several buddies in the Army, and his grandparents. He believed in a merciful Father, but the sight of someone hurting to get to the other side was disturbing and heartbreaking.

Finally, the shower shut off, but he kept up his pacing. He woke at five a.m. every day to push himself for an hour in the gym, then let himself escape the house. With his trusted security personnel notified that he was gone, he would go on an hour-long run outside, up in the mountains or down through the scenic town. The physical outlet and escape from the beautiful prison helped, but he needed more intense activity if he was going to allow himself to stay so close to Kaytlyn.

The bedroom door opened, and Kaytlyn stood there. Even with her face pale and the weight she'd lost, she was still breathtakingly beautiful. She wore a simple white sundress that showed off the creamy skin of her neck and shoulders far too much. What he wouldn't give to simply touch that skin, maybe press his lips to it. Oh man. He'd try to lie to himself and say today was worse than usual, but every day of the past two months had been just as excruciating.

"Hey," she whispered, smiling up at him.

"Hey." His voice was too deep and husky. She had to know how she affected him. Anyone could read through the lines and see his stupid, desperate, secret love. He swallowed hard and said, "Can you walk?" Most of him prayed she would say yes, but there was a small, rebellious part of him that screamed for her to say, *No, carry me, Cameron.* Sheesh, he was a pathetic, weak mess.

She nodded bravely. "It'll be good for me."

He loved how strong and brave she was. He'd never seen someone as sick as she and Jacob were. At least Kaytlyn's sickness had an end in sight. He frowned. Jacob's sickness would end too, but not in a way any of them wanted to see. Yet Cameron didn't want to watch Jacob hurt any longer. He also really needed something to change with him and Kaytlyn, or he might have to break his vow to Jacob to protect her and beg Sutton to send someone to replace him. No. He couldn't stand the thought of even one of his trusted friends close to this delicate yet tough woman. This was his job, and he wasn't giving it up for anyone or anything.

They walked slowly down the hallway. He didn't touch her or even look at her, but he was hyperaware of her every movement. Her delicate features were etched into his mind.

"Today seems like a bad one," he said into the silence.

"For me or Jacob?"

"Both." He let himself look at her. Her blond hair was a deep honey as it was still wet, trailing down her back. Even weak and sickly, she glided along and glowed. "You okay?"

"I just wish it was over."

His brow furrowed. "Over?" She couldn't mean ...

"The morning sickness."

"Oh." He cleared his throat and said, "I thought twelve weeks ..."

"Me too, and that was yesterday." She tenderly placed her hand over her abdomen. "The doctor said sometimes fourteen. At least I never had to be hospitalized or get an IV."

"That is good." Cameron felt like patting himself on the back. He was doing well so far: normal conversation, not too many longing looks, and absolutely no physical contact. He might make it through one more day in this limbo of being near Kaytlyn, but not near enough.

They reached Jacob's door. Cameron reached for the knob but paused. "Ready?"

Kaytlyn focused on him. The power in those blue eyes was incredible. "How bad is he?"

Cameron winced. She hadn't been here for a few days. "Pretty bad."

"Cam."

He sucked in a breath. The way she said his name like that, a nickname, was almost a caress. "Yes?" he managed.

"Thank you for being here."

He nodded, unable to speak with her looking at him like he was her hero or something.

"No matter what ... you'll be here?"

This he could promise. "No matter what, Kayt." He let himself have the privilege of using her nickname in return. He'd only slipped once before, that first day she was sick when she hadn't answered her phone or her door and he'd been so concerned. Since then, he only thought of her as his Kayt in his mind. Yet she'd pulled the nickname card a few seconds ago, and he figured turnabout was fair play.

She squared her shoulders and said, "Okay, I'm ready."

Cameron badly wanted to do something simple like rest his hand on the small of her back to direct her in, sweep her off her feet so she didn't have to walk, or kiss her until she knew exactly how committed he was to protecting her. He shook his head to clear it again, swung the door open, and waited for her to walk into the suite.

Usually, Jacob had all the windows uncovered, and throughout his and Kaytlyn's sicknesses, the housekeepers had done an incredible job of keeping their rooms spotless. For the past few days, the suite had been as dark as a tomb; Jacob had finally admitted the light was giving him an unbearable headache. It was still clean, but there was a smell that Cameron had learned to loathe in the military—the smell of death. Jacob's death wasn't coming from an external force; he was wasting away from the inside out. Cameron hated it.

His eyes were closed, and he didn't acknowledge them as they came in. Cameron left the hallway door open so the light would filter in. Jacob's breathing was labored; he wasn't resting peacefully. Kaytlyn sank into the chair at his bedside. Cameron stood next to her.

They waited in the unbearable silence for maybe half a minute. Jacob struggled with each breath and his eyes were shut tight, as if he was squeezing them shut to keep out something.

"He doesn't look like himself," Kaytlyn finally murmured.

"No," Cameron agreed.

Jacob's skin now hung on his bones. His eyebrows had dipped over his eyes until the sockets were barely visible. The veins in his arms and hands popped through translucent skin. Cameron hurt just watching this extraordinary man waste away.

Kaytlyn's eyes were bright and bluer than ever. She brushed her fingers across Jacob's brow.

His eyes opened. He stared at the ceiling for a second, then painstakingly turned his head to the side and focused on Kaytlyn. "Ah, Kayt," he ground out slowly.

"Jacob." She gave him a brave smile.

"You look ... sick," he said.

Kaytlyn laughed, brushing at the tears spilling over onto her cheeks. "You don't look any better, my friend."

Jacob gave what might've been a chuckle, but it must've hurt as he released her hand and clasped his own to his chest.

"Jacob?" Kaytlyn's voice pitched with concern.

"It's time," he said firmly.

"Are you sure?" Kaytlyn sounded terrified, more uncertain than Cameron had ever seen her.

Jacob smiled as his eyes traced over her face. "I couldn't be more proud of you. You're going to do great things ..." His eyes moved to Cameron's face. "Together."

Kaytlyn's gaze also darted up to Cameron.

"Protect her," Jacob said.

Cameron nodded, as serious as when he'd been baptized a Christian or taken the oath of enlistment. "With my life."

"Thank you." He focused back on Kaytlyn. "Protect our legacy, and our baby."

Cameron loved how his friend had taken Kaytlyn's baby as his own. He despised the truth of the baby's paternity and worried if he saw Peter he'd strangle him, but it didn't matter to Jacob. Kaytlyn's child was Jacob's heir on paper and in his heart.

Tears splashed down her cheeks, and she had a rough time getting the words out. "I will."

"I love you, sweet Kayt."

"I love you too," she managed to say.

Jacob gave her one more smile, and then he closed his eyes. The room stilled, and the only sound was Kaytlyn's soft cry as Jacob took his last breath. Cameron knew he was gone, yet he'd left a legacy of a life lived for everyone else. Moisture ran down his own cheeks, and he quickly brushed it away.

Kaytlyn didn't scream or sob as he'd thought she might. She laid her cheek against the side of Jacob's head, closed her eyes tightly, and let the tears run unchecked down her cheeks.

Cameron stood there helplessly with his hands clasped behind his back. He couldn't protect her from this. The clock was the only sound in the room besides their breathing.

Second after second ticked by, and Kaytlyn didn't move. Finally, she raised her head, gave Jacob a soft kiss on the cheek, and used the bed to stand. Her legs gave out. Cameron caught her around the waist and for once didn't fight his instinct to pull her close. He swept her off her feet and against his chest. She weighed next to nothing, yet he'd never had anything so substantial and important in his arms.

Kaytlyn's eyes were red-rimmed. She stared at him for half a beat and said, "Have you got me?"

Cameron nodded. "Always."

Kaytlyn gave him a watery smile and laid her head against his chest. "Thank you." She didn't say anything more. Cameron let his eyes trail over the lifeless body of his friend and boss. He swallowed at the emotion creeping up. Jacob was gone. Kaytlyn needed him.

Turning, he strode from the room with her clinging to his neck. He had imagined he'd feel a guilty sort of relief when Jacob passed, but it was the exact opposite. He felt sorrow at losing his friend, a loss that would make the world a worse place, as Jacob was a benevolent rock for so many people. Cameron also felt an impending sense of doom; he feared the next chapter in Kaytlyn's fight would be harder than the last.

He cuddled her even closer, savoring the feel of her in his arms and recommitting to not let her out of his sight. No one was going to hurt her or the baby.

CHAPTER SEVEN

The next three days in the mansion were busy and somber. The entire staff was subdued, and Kaytlyn often saw tears in their eyes. Everyone had loved and almost revered Jacob. She knew exactly how they felt. Miraculously, her nausea eased. While it wasn't gone, she was able to get up the day after Jacob's passing, eat her toast and drink her ginger tea, shower, and make it to her office with Cameron anxiously trailing behind her as if she would collapse.

The thought of Cameron had her smiling to herself as she worked out funeral plans, sent announcements to media correspondents, and dealt with emails and texts of friends and associates sending their condolences. While no one but her, Cameron, Larry, and the doctor knew of their marriage or the baby, everyone knew how close she and Jacob had been. She cried off and on throughout the days leading up to the funeral, but she made it through them.

Cameron had stationed himself just outside her office or bedroom door, only leaving her when she slept. He was there for her, but he was still detached. He'd held her close and carried her to her room after Jacob's passing, but he hadn't touched her since or said much to her besides constantly asking how she was doing. He was a lot more than just a set of strong arms to hold her up. She knew he would be there for her, in sickness or in health, no matter what. Her respect and trust for him just kept growing.

The morning of the funeral was a gorgeous, bright blue August day. Kaytlyn dressed in a silky, short-sleeved knee-length black dress. There was a little more color in her cheeks today, and she didn't feel quite as gaunt, as she'd been able to keep food down since Jacob passed. He must be watching over her from heaven. She'd always believed in God and an afterlife, but she'd never felt His existence quite so deeply as she did now.

Swinging open her bedroom door, she paused and admired the sight of Cameron standing there in a black suit. He was so handsome that he stole her breath away. His gaze traveled over her carefully. He didn't smile, but his blue eyes warmed. "You look beautiful, Kayt," he murmured.

"So do you," she said, noticing he'd used her nickname again. She loved it on his lips. She'd love a lot more from his lips, but now was not the time to be indulging in selfish fantasies.

He did smile then. "Take it back."

Kaytlyn grinned, loving that he could tease even for a second. "Pretty boy," she shot at him.

"Gorgeous girl," he shot back.

"Ooh, what an insult." She laughed.

Cameron chuckled with her. They sobered at the same time, and Cameron stared at her. "It feels good to laugh," he said.

"There hasn't been much to laugh about for a while now. Is it going to get easier, Cam? Are we going to laugh and be happy again?"

"Yes. I'll make sure your life gets easier and you can laugh and be happy."

Kaytlyn felt his declaration deeply, but even as tough and amazing as Cameron was, she didn't know that anyone could make her life easier and happier for the time being. She was a pregnant widow of a well-known billionaire philanthropist, and when her former best friend found out that Kaytlyn owned everything and the will had been changed—not to mention that Kaytlyn had married Jacob and the child Jessica thought would be hers was being claimed as Jacob's heir—all of the devil's minions would be loosed.

Cameron lifted his hand, and her eyes widened. So many times, he'd almost touched her but then stopped himself. Would he stop today? His hand seemed to be in slow motion as it covered the distance, and then he simply cradled her cheek in his palm.

Kaytlyn leaned into his touch, bringing her own hand up to wrap around his. "It feels good to be touched," she said, hoping he wouldn't pull away.

His eyes got serious. "Kayt. I promised Jacob ... we have to take things slow."

Kaytlyn didn't know exactly what that meant or what he'd

promised Jacob, but though she longed to be closer to Cameron, she was in no rush. There was too much to deal with right now, and it wasn't like she had time for something so sweet as romance. But oh, how she craved it—no, she craved him.

Yet she knew how determined Cameron was, and she would need time to heal from Jacob's loss. She didn't know what else to say but, "All right."

Cameron gave her a tight smile, removed his hand, and gestured down the hall. Kaytlyn squared her shoulders and walked in front of him.

The limousine took them to the graveside service. Cameron stayed close by her side, and although he didn't touch her, his sheer strength and presence felt protective and comforting. He was her friend and support, exactly what she needed. She had a hard time focusing as people gave their speeches: the governor of Idaho; one of Jacob's longtime friends, who was now a general in the Army; an associate who headed the anti-trafficking battle in South America; and finally Larry, who said a few words as Jacob's close friend and church leader.

There was a huge crowd, and unfortunately, Jessica and Peter had been seated right next to Cameron and Kaytlyn. Kaytlyn ignored Jessica's sneaky dagger looks and Peter's fake classy act. It still hurt that someone she'd been close to could betray her like Jessica did but she could feel Jessica's hatred for her. It oozed from the woman. Kaytlyn kept her shoulders and back straight, her head tilted up, and her hands carefully folded in her lap.

When the 21-gun salute was finished and Larry gave a benediction, the local National Guard folded up the flag covering the casket and marched as a unit up to Kaytlyn. The soldier leading the color guard formally handed over the flag. With tears clouding her vision, Kaytlyn pulled the flag tightly against her chest.

The quiet hush over the crowd was broken by a wail of outrage. "Why are you giving the flag to her? I am my father's only living relative!" Jessica shrieked.

The entire crowd drew in a breath. Cameron wrapped his arm around Kaytlyn as if to shield her. Kaytlyn wanted to just run back to the mansion and never have to deal with this woman, but it was time. The silence was so thick and heavy, it felt more oppressive than the warm August day. Kaytlyn was strong, though. She had been trained by Jacob how to be poised and gracious, and how to stand up for herself.

Every eye at the service was focused on Kaytlyn. She didn't focus on Jessica but gave Peter an imperious look. "I am Jacob Tarbet's widow, am carrying his child, and am the sole recipient of his estate." Maybe she shouldn't have thrown that last statement in there, and the middle one wasn't true, but she might as well hit them with everything at once.

The silence after her statement was deafening. No one in the crowd so much as shifted their weight. Peter's eyes narrowed and he focused on Kaytlyn as if determining how much of an adversary she was.

Jessica fell against her husband, her eyes widening in shock. Two seconds later, she went berserk. She started screaming insults at Kaytlyn, flailing in her husband's arms to try to get at Kaytlyn, and making a scene worse than any spoiled toddler could dream of. Surprisingly, she said nothing about the baby, it was all about Kaytlyn stealing her inheritance and many references to Kaytlyn being a "tramp".

Cameron released his hold on Kaytlyn, stepped in front of her, and in a voice as sharp as a whip commanded, "Stop speaking or I will cut your tongue out."

Jessica drew back from him with a look of horror. Kaytlyn supposed that if you didn't know about Cameron's good heart, he would look terrifying. His build was strong, and the years of being in command in the military etched lines of authority into his face.

"Escort her out of here," Cameron commanded.

The security team surrounded Jessica and Peter. Peter pivoted quickly to go, putting up no fuss. Kaytlyn thought that was smart of him. She knew Cameron wanted an excuse to go after the man and Cameron could easily tear him apart.

Peter was a politician in public. Always. He would most likely be livid with Jessica's outbursts today. Back when they were friends, Kaytlyn hadn't liked how Peter seemed to control Jessica, but now she knew Jacob's daughter was no better than her slimy husband. They both wielded their power behind the scenes, sneakily. This was the first open attack Kaytlyn had ever seen or heard of. She'd blindsided Jessica and Peter, just like Jacob had planned.

Jessica didn't speak again, breaking from her husband's grip and storming ahead of Kaytlyn's security personnel. The crowd watched them go. After they finally loaded into their Tesla and sped away, there was a collective sigh and the murmuring began.

Cameron's fierce gaze softened as he turned to Kaytlyn. "Are you okay?"

She waved one hand at the onlookers while clutching the flag in the other. "You think I care what that piece of work thinks of me?"

A smile broke over his face and Kaytlyn felt her knees almost buckle. He was so handsome that it took her breath away. He looked like he wanted to hug her as badly as she wanted to hug him, but the crowd was pressing in to offer their condolences. Cameron took the flag from her, sticking close enough to discourage anyone from so much as looking at her wrong. No one did. Hundreds of people came by to press her hand, share a kind remembrance of Jacob, or give her a hug. Many asked about the baby, but everybody was too classy to give voice to the unspoken questions: When had she and Jacob married, and why had she married a man thirty years her senior who had always appeared to be only her friend and business partner? Most of them probably thought it was for the money. Many of them probably felt bad for Jessica, as few had insight into how demented she was.

Finally, the crowd dwindled. Kaytlyn had been feeling stronger today, but now she was close to collapse.

Cameron discreetly put a steadying hand on her lower back. "What do you need?" he asked.

You. Sadly, she couldn't say that. Not yet. They both needed time to mourn Jacob and get through whatever Peter and Jessica were going to hurl at them. Larry and Jacob had felt that this course would protect her baby, the businesses, the money, and the foundation, but Kaytlyn still had a sense of foreboding that she wanted to push away. "Would you be shocked if I told you I'm craving a Grumpy's hamburger and fries?"

He grinned. "I'd say that's the best news I've heard in a while." He nodded to their security team, who cleared a path through the remaining crowd to a couple of Porsche sport utilities. "We're going through the Grumpy's drive-through," Cameron said to Tyler, a young guy who always had a smile on his face.

"Yes!" Tyler pumped his eyebrows at Kaytlyn. "I like the way you think."

"Thanks." Kaytlyn waved to and smiled at the people who were watching them go, keeping her composure as Jacob had trained her to. As Cameron helped her into the back of the vehicle and settled in next to her, she was exhausted, but she'd made it through. Jacob was gone. It was time to somehow face the future without him.

CHAPTER EIGHT

Cameron had been raised to respect and revere women, but he'd never been so tempted to hit a woman as when he'd faced Jacob's daughter at the funeral. His blood still boiled thinking of Jessica calling sweet, angelic Kaytlyn a tramp. All the while her loser husband stood there trying to appear dignified and unruffled.

They'd gone through the drive-through, eaten in the car, and had now arrived home. Kaytlyn had only eaten half of the bacon cheeseburger and a few fries, but at least she'd eaten. He just kept getting more invested in this woman, as if his purpose in life was to protect and love her. Jacob's caution to take it slow kept ringing in his ears. He would listen but it wouldn't be easy.

Hours had passed, and the shadows of evening crept in. Kaytlyn was resting in her room, but Cameron felt so restless he could hardly stand it. He wanted to exercise—no, he wanted to punch something, or someone. Sadly he hadn't been gifted with an excuse to punch Peter at the funeral. If only Peter would've been the one to start hurling insults at Kaytlyn. Smashing that man's perfect face would help right so many wrongs.

Maybe one of his security guys would spar with him while Kaytlyn slept. He almost called to let the security office know he'd be away from Kaytlyn's door for a bit and they needed to send someone to sit with her.

Suddenly, her door sprang open. Her hair was mussed and her eyes looked heavy. She was still wearing that silky black dress that hugged her curves. He would've thought losing so much weight would make her lose those curves, but the pregnancy was filling her out in all the right spots. His stomach swirled with desire for her, and he wondered if he could bend, or more likely break, the "taking it slow" rule by sweeping her off her feet and kissing her until neither of them could catch a breath.

"Larry needs to meet with us," she said shortly.

Cameron's fantasies all popped, and he stepped back, letting her go ahead. They walked through the wide hall toward the main staircase. "Is everything okay?" he asked.

"Apparently, they're already filing suits."

"That was quick. Do you know what they're claiming?"

She shook her head.

Jessica had only found out that she'd lost her inheritance this morning and Peter should be trying to cover his butt after unethically using Kaytlyn's egg without her permission. They shouldn't have any quick or easy recourse in Cameron's mind.

They strode down the staircase and into Kaytlyn's office. Kaytlyn stood behind the desk, biting at her lip and looking so small and uncertain, he wanted to cradle her close. The doorbell rang, and half a minute later, one of his security guys escorted Larry in. Kaytlyn and Cameron each shook his hand; then he gestured for them to sit, and they both did.

Larry was a tall man with short, curly hair and a slight stoop. His green eyes were sharp but kind.

"How bad is it?" Kaytlyn asked, perching on the edge of the chair. Obviously, her mind had been going to worst-case scenarios. Cameron should've reassured her somehow.

"Well ... Jessica's pressing a suit against Cameron for threatening her."

Cameron guffawed at that. "Bring it on." He was secretly pleased, though. If he took the heat off of Kaytlyn, that would be great.

"But she's also digging deep and going at this from every angle. I'm not worried," Larry reassured her quickly. "Everything is already in your name. We're solid. We just have to make sure everything is in line to fight the stuff she's trying to throw at you. Their lawyer, Bridget, is a friend of mine—"

"Why would a friend of yours represent them?" Cameron asked.

"You have to understand that most people like and respect Jessica and Peter." He tilted his head. "I always liked her— thought of her as an adopted niece, honestly—until Jacob revealed what she'd said to him and broke his heart in the process."

Cameron nodded. He'd met people in the military who were like Jessica and Peter: they told you exactly what you wanted to hear, smiled while they did it, and then stabbed you in the back.

"Because her lawyer and I are friends, we have a lot more information than we normally would," Larry continued.

Cameron's eyebrows arched.

"Don't get me wrong. This is an important case, and Bridget wants to win. She's a with-it lawyer, and she loves Jessica and believes everything she's telling her. Honestly, a lot of people were upset with Kaytlyn today for blindsiding Jessica at her father's funeral."

Cameron hadn't thought of it like that; it made sense. If they thought highly of Jacob and Jessica, they could think of Kaytlyn as a scheming outsider.

"I think Bridget actually shared so much to pretend to buddy up to me. She doesn't know how deceitful Jessica is, and she thinks I'm only representing you out of loyalty to Jacob. But most of this info and the suits they're filing are more of a scare tactic, hoping you'll get scared and settle. Maybe they think that I'm getting old and don't want to fight. There's only one matter that's a huge concern for us. So let's just plug through what they're claiming and what we need to do."

Kaytlyn nodded for him to proceed. Cameron wanted to know what the one huge concern was.

"Of course it's all about the money and they're claiming you two are lovers and threatened and manipulated Jacob into changing the will on his deathbed."

Cameron rolled his eyes. Of course they had no clue how hard Cameron had fought to not act on his love for Kaytlyn. Everything Jacob had done was to protect Kaytlyn from Peter and Jessica.

"I think we'll be fine there," Larry reassured. "The will was changed and all of the business and assets were transferred two months ago, definitely not on his deathbed. I can get witnesses that you two have never manipulated or threatened Jacob. The more concerning thing, and it's a big one ..." Larry looked down. "They have proof that you knew it was your egg, and you signed away the rights to the baby."

"No." Kaytlyn rocked to her feet, horrified. "No," she repeated as if that would make it true.

Larry pulled out some papers and set them in front of Kaytlyn. She looked them over then pushed them away with a shaky hand. "I trusted them," she muttered.

Cameron's gut clenched. So it was her signature.

"They told me I had to sign to be a surrogate. I had no idea ..." Her face was pale. She sank back into the chair. "They can't have my baby," she said fiercely.

Larry nodded. "I know. We're going to fight them. There have been cases where the judge has ruled in favor of the surrogate. The judge will have the final call after their evaluation of your mental state, your relationship with Jacob will come into play, your current relationships," he glanced at Cameron, "and how strong your claim to the child is."

"It's my child," Kaytlyn replied heatedly, cradling her arms across her abdomen as if to protect the baby.

Oh, how Cameron wanted to soothe her. After Larry left, if she let him, he'd hold her and find a way to make all of this right. Yet he was only a simple soldier, and this wasn't something he could win with fists or battle tactics. Instinctively, he thought there was no court that would take a woman's baby away, and there was no way they could prove Kaytlyn would be an unfit mother. Yet she'd signed the baby away, unknowingly, but it was still there.

"I believe we can win. For sure with the will and possibly with the baby."

"They can take the money." Kaytlyn covered her abdomen with her hands.

Cameron loved her. Of course the baby was all she cared about.

"It's okay," Larry reassured. "We can win both. We just have to make sure everything's in line, and you'll have to go on the stand and testify that you didn't know you were signing your baby away. Our chances are great. I have some ideas to make the unfit mother thing even harder for her to prove and prove Peter's infidelity and Jessica's instability." Larry placed a hand over Kaytlyn's. "Jacob was one of my closest friends and the man I most admired out of everyone in the world. I'm going to fight for you and the baby."

Cameron felt marginally better. Larry was a respected lawyer. Hopefully, Jessica and Peter would have no case. Maybe they'd get awarded some money and disappear. He could hope so, as the thought of them taking Kaytlyn's baby was horrific. He'd give them all the money and vote for Peter himself if it could somehow prevent handing Kaytlyn's innocent child over. If it came to that, he'd take his ten million and hide Kaytlyn away in some foreign country where they'd never find her.

"I have to show you some of the evidence she has," Larry said.

Larry started spreading pictures across the desk and explaining them. There were pictures of Cameron and Kaytlyn on the hikes they used to take, time-stamped to show they were taken while she was married to Jacob. One showed him holding her close. The truth was that she'd tripped and almost fallen, and he'd grabbed her and lifted her up to protect her.

Even worse, there were pictures of him carrying Kaytlyn from Jacob's room to her bedroom the day Jacob had died. It looked like he was carrying her straight to bed.

"How did she get these?" Cameron demanded. Those would have to be from the security cameras. No, the angles weren't right. With all the windows in the mansion, they could be from outside.

Kaytlyn was staring at the pictures in concern.

Larry shook his head. "A drone?"

At least he didn't have a leak in his security team. He'd have to look at their sensors, though, and make sure a drone couldn't get through them from above. It wasn't a threat he'd considered. "How did she know to be compiling all of this?" Cameron asked.

Larry arched his brows. "From what I dug out of her lawyer." He smiled grimly. "Jessica has despised Kaytlyn for a long time and was planning to go after the foundation and the fifty million that

Kaytlyn was promised in the original will as soon as Jacob passed. So she's been assembling her arsenal. And maybe she was afraid Jacob would pull something like this after her fit."

Kaytlyn shook her head. "She thought she was inheriting billions, but she couldn't stand the thought of me getting anything?"

"Her hatred seems to run deep." Larry pulled out more pictures. "The pictures get worse."

Cameron stared. There was a picture of Kaytlyn shooting a needle into her own arm, partially concealed by a bunch of pine trees. It was followed by a picture of Kaytlyn handing over money and taking a bag of what appeared to be cocaine. Maybe at a park?

"What?" Cameron exploded, jumping to his feet. "How could she possibly doctor something like this?" He knew some photographic experts might be able to do this, but it looked so real.

"She didn't doctor it." Kaytlyn's voice squeaked, and her face was contorted in pain.

Cameron's stomach dropped as he turned to her. No. He couldn't believe that Kaytlyn would be shooting up or buying cocaine. There was no way to wrap his mind around the incredible woman he knew doing that to herself or breaking the law like that. He squinted at the picture. She looked much younger; maybe she'd had a problem before?

"It's my sister," Kaytlyn said quietly. "People always used to say how we looked like twins."

Cameron sank back into his chair. "We can prove that, then."

"Hopefully," Larry said. "She's also got signed affidavits from household staff, claiming they've seen Kaytlyn throwing fits and breaking things, threatening Jacob, et cetera."

"But that's all slander," Cameron said, hating the hurt look in Kaytlyn's eyes. Who on the staff would do that to Kaytlyn? Yet there were some who had been with Jacob for many years, and they might be more loyal to Jessica, the girl they'd raised, than to Kaytlyn, the outsider who came in and took everything over.

"It's their word against ours. I'm sure we can get many character witnesses for Kaytlyn." Larry gave her a kind smile. "There was also a reference to your father being abusive."

Kaytlyn blinked and then looked away. "Emotionally, he was."

"No one can blame you for that, but it gives more validation to the picture she's trying to paint if you were abused as a child and ran from that, only to run to Jacob. Plus there's the statistics of those who are abused not breaking the cycle." Larry shrugged.

Cameron despised how this was digging at Kaytlyn, and he could only imagine how awful she was feeling. He wanted to move on, do something positive. "Is there anything we can do besides getting our own character witnesses and disproving these?" Cameron gestured to the pictures and papers on the desk.

"Yeah." Larry turned his wizened gaze on Kaytlyn. "But Kaytlyn, first I want to promise you we're going to fight all of this. We have a good chance. We've just got to make sure we have everything in line. She most likely has more 'evidence' that we haven't seen, but our case is strong. I don't want you to worry."

Cameron wondered if Larry really believed that, or if he was just trying to make Kaytlyn feel better so she didn't get overwhelmed and put stress on the baby. Yet there had to be a way to prove she hadn't signed away her baby on purpose. Cameron would do anything to help her prove she was a fit mother and if she'd let him he'd help her raise the child.

"But most people believe anything Jessica and Peter say," Kaytlyn pointed out. "And in this small town, more than likely the judge was also Jessica's piano teacher."

Cameron couldn't help but grimace at that. It was a tight-knit town, but a lot of new blood and new money was pouring in, changing the populace to an extent.

"Jessica and Peter are very highly esteemed, but so was Jacob, and you can't discount how polished and with-it you are and all the good you've done in the community," Larry pointed out.

"Thank you."

Cameron agreed. If anyone could look into Jessica's eyes and not see evil, they weren't looking hard enough. On the flip side, if they could look into Kaytlyn's eyes and not see an angel, they weren't living right. But that wouldn't matter to a judge who was relying on only facts, not emotion.

"We're going to be fine. If Jessica can find people on our staff willing to lie, you can bet I'll find people on their staff willing to tell the truth." Larry arched an eyebrow. "I already have a friend in the Idaho Senate who told me some truths about Peter, his women, and his type of politics. Not that he's an anomaly in this day and age of dirty politics, but the judge still won't like it. I also have another idea that will make our case even stronger, and I don't think it'll be that big of a deal."

"Okay." Kaytlyn looked to Cameron as if drawing strength from him. He wanted to squeeze her hand to encourage her, but he settled for smiling.

"I need you to get engaged," Larry said.

Cameron's smile disappeared. What was Larry thinking? She'd recently been widowed.

"Excuse me?" Kaytlyn put a hand to her chest and sat back. "Get engaged?"

"Jessica claims that you're a drug user, and the employees are saying you're unstable and prone to anger. She claims she and Peter can give the baby a stable home, a mother and a father." He rolled his eyes. "If you can find the right man to be engaged to—someone solid, easygoing, with a good reputation—your overall case with everything from the businesses to the baby will be stronger. We'll get all our ducks in a row with everything else, and Jessica will be begging us for a settlement much smaller than the fifty million of yours she thought she was going after before Jacob axed her completely, and she'll never touch your child." Larry smiled in encouragement. "Can you think of someone to get engaged to?"

Me! Cameron wanted to stand up, throw his hand in the air, and shout it. He was the right man. It was perfect. Was this the sign from heaven Jacob was going to send? They could get engaged and get married, Cameron could raise Kaytlyn's baby as his own, and they could finally be together. The idea made him happier than he'd been in a long while.

Kaytlyn said nothing, but her eyes swung to Cameron, and he could read the longing and hope there just as surely as she could see it in his own. His heart thudded faster and faster, and he knew that no matter what Jessica and Peter threw at them, they could take it if they stuck together.

"Not you," Larry said to Cameron, bringing all his dreams to a crushing halt as he easily guessed Cameron's intentions.

"Why not?" Cameron rounded on him. "It *has* to be me. I would never trust anyone else with Kaytlyn, and I refuse to let anyone else close enough to her to pretend they're engaged."

Larry was shaking his head. "I'm sorry, Cameron. You saw the pictures she has of the two of you. She's claiming all kinds of twisted things you two did to Jacob. She's saying you two schemed up the marriage and forced poor Jacob into gifting his companies and rewriting the will so you could then wait for him to die and have everything of his, and steal she and Peter's child in the process."

"The lady is insane," Cameron protested. "What judge is going to listen to that?" *Not you, not you.* Larry's voice was harsh in his head. He didn't think he could handle looking at Kaytlyn. What if she was okay with it not being him? What if she wanted to be engaged to some other yahoo? It had been hard enough watching her be married to Jacob, and they'd never even kissed each other or had any sort of romantic exchanges or intentions. Did she have someone in mind? Any man would jump at the chance to be close to Kaytlyn. Would she ditch Cameron like a used-up bullet casing and move on? His chest was so tight he could hardly catch a breath.

"I've been around a long time, and I'm not going to lie, I've seen some crazy stuff, but I feel good about our chances of winning.

I'm not as concerned about the money, but I want to do everything I can to prevent them from getting the baby."

Cameron had very recently thought he'd also do anything for Kaytlyn and the baby. Why did the thought of her being engaged to someone else seem to be too much? He'd dealt with her being married to Jacob. But Jacob had never touched her ... kissed her. His stomach rolled.

"Kaytlyn, can you think of a close friend who has a good reputation, hopefully someone you've dated in the past, who would fake an engagement with you? It wouldn't have to be a big deal, maybe some pictures that we send to the media, but it will kill Jessica's angle with you and Cameron, and it will make you look more stable so her unfit mother nonsense is weaker too."

Cameron forced himself to look at her and see what she was thinking. If she had somebody in mind, it might tear him apart. She stared at him as if afraid he would break; then she focused on Larry. "Yeah, there's someone who might work."

No! Cameron clenched his fists and exercised what he believed was superhuman self-control when he wanted to punch a hole through the wall. No, he wanted to punch a hole through the face of whatever guy Kaytlyn was thinking of. *There's someone who might work.* He prayed that it wouldn't work. *Please, Lord. Please, Jacob. Help me.*

"Great," Larry said like it was no big deal, putting everything back in his laptop bag. "Let me know how it progresses. I'm going to dig into the doctor's office who did the insemination and see if I can find an ally. We can't really disprove the pictures of you two on the hikes, but we can get the ones taken from the drone thrown out. I'll work on proving that it's Kandy in the pictures with the drugs, and I'll get character witnesses for you and some testimonials from Jessica's household staff about how insane she truly is. I've already got some solid dirt on Peter but I'll keep looking." He stood.

Cameron offered his hand to Larry. Though he was concerned and upset at this turn of events, he knew Larry was giving them the best legal advice he could.

"Keep your security guys on their toes," Larry cautioned him. "I wouldn't put it past Peter or Jessica to be using all of this as a smoke screen while they plan something more sinister."

Cameron nodded his agreement. They were both certifiably psychotic. He couldn't believe that anyone would fall for Jessica or Peter's fake exterior, but many people did.

Larry walked out the office door. Cameron didn't even know how to approach Kaytlyn right now. Could he beg her to let him be her fiancé? Who cared what stupid Jessica claimed? They could bring in witness after witness of how mentally stable Jacob was right until the end and how Cameron had never behaved in a manner besides security guard and a friend to Kaytlyn. Yet ... he couldn't put her at risk to lose her baby to those people. He'd have to keep dealing with whatever came at him. No matter how bad it hurt.

"Cam?" Her soft voice pulled him around.

He met her gaze and knew he'd do anything for her. "Yeah?"

"It's going to be okay."

Cameron didn't think so, but it was sweet that she could reassure him despite the mess she was in. He could walk away, and she couldn't—except they both knew he never would walk away from her. He pushed a hand through his hair. "So you have ..." He cleared his throat and muttered, "Someone in mind?"

She pressed her lips together and picked up her phone. "Trey's an old friend. He'll help me if he can."

That was the last thing Cameron wanted to hear. *He* was supposed to help her, not some loser from her past. Trey. He considered where he'd heard that name before, and he remembered a golden boy YouTube joker coming to visit right before Kaytlyn had married Jacob. He'd taken her on a hike and to dinner. The guy had an easy smile and seemed to just enjoy life. He wasn't going to enjoy it when Cameron pummeled him.

Kaytlyn was messaging somebody on her phone. Was it Trey? How long had she dated the guy? How much did she like him? Where was Trey when she was sick every morning? Could the smiley guy truly waltz in here and take away Cameron's happiness?

"So what's the plan?" he managed to ask. He tried to take comfort that Larry had said the fake engagement was no big deal, but it felt like a very big deal to him.

"The pilot is in California taking his kids to Disneyland." Her brow pulled together. "Are you up for a road trip? I'd love to get away from all of this for a few days." She gestured back to her desk. The incriminating pictures and paperwork were gone, but both of them could still see them and what they represented: a nightmarish legal battle over insane claims that should never be proved.

Cameron would love to break away from this mansion, and he'd love to spend hours alone with her in a car. He'd have his security team follow in another vehicle. But letting her travel so she could get fake engaged to some guy? This had the makings of a nightmare.

CHAPTER NINE

Kaytlyn slept through most of the eleven-hour drive to Colorado, which was just as well, because Cameron had gone all stoic and military on her again. They stopped and stayed the night in Boulder, getting two connecting suites at the St. Julien. Kaytlyn didn't sleep well. She should've waited for the pilot to get back from his family vacation, but she really wanted to escape the mansion. She wanted to be far from Peter and Jessica's stupid allegations, from whoever on her staff had accused her of being unstable, and especially from the knowledge that she had signed her baby away. How could Jessica have betrayed her like that? She had to focus on how they were going to fight for her baby because other wise she'd break down.

She'd tried to call her old boyfriend, Trey Nelson, several times, and he hadn't answered. She'd finally gotten through to his best friend, Gavin Strong, and learned that Trey was in their hometown of Lonepeak for the long weekend, doing bike rides and seminars for guests of Gavin's lodge, Angel Falls Retreat. She'd see soon enough if he was up for the ploy, as they were almost there.

Trey was a nice guy, he'd always been a good friend, and most of all, she trusted him. She knew that if there was any way to make it work, he would do it. They'd dated seriously during their senior year of high school, and every time he got close to Sun Valley over the past ten years, he'd come by and see her, take her on a bike ride or a hike or out to dinner. She'd actually gone out with him about a week before she'd gotten pregnant. Trey was also well loved on the internet, to the point that even if people were upset at her getting engaged so quickly, they'd forgive her if she was engaged to someone amazing like Trey.

After driving through the dry parts of Idaho, Utah, and western Colorado, they were finally back to mountains and greenery. Kaytlyn loved her Colorado home. She wanted to go see her mother and sister while she was here, but her last bitter fight with her father kept playing through her mind.

Kaytlyn rarely saw her family, keeping in touch with her youngest sister through texts that constantly begged her to leave home and come live with her. Sadly, Krysta didn't respond beyond one-word answers. Occasionally, Kaytlyn would call her mother, but the words she'd hear over the phone were even less verbose than Krysta's texts.

Kaytlyn had left home at eighteen and gotten as far away as she could until she ran out of fuel for her beater car and only had enough to feed herself for a few days. She'd been hoping to get to the Oregon coast, but as she hit Twin Falls, Idaho, she'd seen an advertisement for Sun Valley and thought it looked like home

—or at least a home without her controlling father. She'd taken the detour, driven into Sun Valley on fumes and a prayer, started working in the first restaurant that hired her, and not long after that she met Jacob. She knew some psychiatrist would say she'd latched on to Jacob because of her lack of a father figure. Whatever. She'd dealt with a father figure for long enough. Jacob had been her best friend, business partner, and her equal, not her father.

Three years ago, she and Jacob had meetings in Vail, so they'd driven to Lonepeak valley to say hello to her family. When she and Jacob had stopped at the run-down family home and ranch, the visit had started semi-cordially. Though she could see the questions in her parents' eyes about her and Jacob's relationship. Then Jacob had made the mistake of offering to give them some money for the ranch and for her sister Kandy's drug rehab. Her father had gone ballistic, calling Kaytlyn a sellout hooker and Jacob a predator. Kaytlyn was certain the men would come to blows, but luckily Jacob was mature enough to walk away. She'd tried to get Krysta to leave with her, but her little sister had only been seventeen at the time and her dad wouldn't let her go.

She hadn't been back. She could just imagine what her father would say about her now, pregnant and alone. At least she had Cameron. She sighed. Or she thought she had Cameron. He'd been dealing so well with the last few months of their odd relationship. He'd been amazing as her protector while she was married to another man, but now the thought of her engaged to someone else was shredding him from the inside out, and she didn't know how to approach the subject. The engagement would hopefully just be some pictures, not a big deal like Larry said. She wished she knew how to approach the subject and get him talking to her about it.

They pulled into her beautiful valley, and she sighed. It was picture perfect. Downtown was decorated with tree-lined, wide streets and quant little shops, all cookie cutter with individual light posts and a faux wrought-iron railing on the second story. Houses and farms like the one her parents lived on were spread throughout the valley, and on the far side loomed the huge lodge, villas, spa, and ski resort, all run by the Strong family.

"Where to?" Cameron asked.

She pointed. "The ski resort up there. That's where he'll be."

Cameron grunted and kept driving. "Who is this joker, anyway?"

"My friend, Trey Nelson."

"Mountain bike and ski trickster?"

So he already knew who Trey was and had been stewing about it. "Yeah." She looked out the window before admitting, "You've seen him at the house before. He stops by to visit and take me out when he's near Sun Valley."

"You're sure he's a ... good guy?"

Kaytlyn wished she could see past his sunglasses and his tough exterior, get a glimpse into those blue eyes she loved so much. She appreciated how much he cared. He was so protective and yet tender. She really needed him right now. "Trey's a good guy. I've known him my whole life."

"And do you want to be engaged to him?"

Kaytlyn sighed. No, she wanted to be engaged to Cameron. Did she tell him that? Would that break down his stoic wall? It really wasn't fair for her to say that, though, and then force him to watch her pretend to be engaged to Trey. "He'll be the best choice."

Cameron's grip tightened on the steering wheel.

"He's a good friend. I'm comfortable with him, and I trust him. He's got a huge social media presence, so we can get it out to the world easily. Plus he travels nonstop, so he can go on with his life, I can go on with mine, and we can just get some pictures out occasionally. When we win against Peter and Jessica, we can quietly break up."

"You make it sound like it's no big deal."

Kaytlyn put her hand on his arm. It was the first time she'd touched him since the funeral, and she savored the feel of his warm, solid flesh under her fingertips. "It isn't a big deal, Cam. We'll get through this." As long as she didn't lose the baby, or Cameron, she could deal with anything else.

They pulled into the parking lot of the resort, and he put it in gear. The other security guys parked a little ways down, leaving a few cars between them so it didn't look like they had added protection. Kaytlyn didn't love having a whole team keeping an eye on them—Cameron was more than capable of taking care of her—but she knew Jessica would stop at nothing to get her money. She put a hand on her stomach; it was still flat, but she knew her baby was in there and growing stronger and bigger each day. She would never let Jessica touch her child.

Cameron took his sunglasses off. His somber eyes flitted down to her hand, then up to her face. "This is killing me, Kayt," he admitted.

Kaytlyn's heart leapt. She knew he still cared, but the past couple of days had killed her as well. "I wish we could change it."

He looked like he wanted to say something, but he shook his head and gave her a sad smile. "We'll get through it." He repeated her words.

"I need to go in there alone," she said.

"We have to watch over you."

"Send the other guys in, and you wait in the car."

Cameron let out a growl of frustration, but he nodded. "Fine." He pulled out his phone and spoke some commands into it. He would stay in the vehicle, but the other men would quietly and unobtrusively enter the lodge before she did, and they'd monitor everything until she was back in the vehicle. She appreciated him for listening, as she could guess that he really didn't want to see her with Trey.

He swung out of the door, hurried around, and helped her out of the car. Stepping back respectfully, he kept his eyes on her. "Be careful," he murmured.

Kaytlyn stepped right up to him, went on tiptoes, and kissed his cheek. She heard his breath catch, and then he released the door, wrapped his arms around her, and pulled her in tight. Kaytlyn wanted to kiss him on the lips, but she forced herself to enjoy just being close and not yearn for more. The timing was not right for them. Would it ever be?

He finally released her and stepped back again. Kaytlyn forced a smile and strode inside. She probably looked worn out and rumpled from driving so long and how sick she'd been the past three months. She was grateful she was finally feeling better. Now she just needed to get through this meeting with Trey. She didn't want to be engaged to anyone but Cameron, even if it was fake, but she would do what she had to do to protect her baby.

Cameron watched Kaytlyn go. His stomach was rolling, his head hurt, and his neck was hot. Was this how morning sickness felt? His sympathy for Kaytlyn doubled. She was so brave, amazing, and impressive, dealing with this for six weeks. He hated letting her go meet with some old boyfriend to propose a fake engagement. He could barely sit here. He wanted to stride into that lodge, push that guy out of the way, kiss her senseless, and then demand she marry him. They could deal with Jessica's slander together.

He banged his head back against the headrest, waited as long as he could stand, and pulled out his phone to call Tyler. "Report," he barked.

"She's gone into a private office with the guy."

No, no, no. He didn't want her alone with some guy. Maybe she trusted the man, but Cameron didn't. How could he trust any man alone with Kaytlyn? What was he doing sitting here? He burst out of the car, ready to go snatch her from that private office.

"Sir?" he heard through the phone he was still clinging to. "How do you want us to proceed?"

Cameron gritted his teeth and stopped in his tracks. He trusted Kaytlyn. He had to. She'd asked him to stay in the car for a reason—probably because she knew he'd rip the guy apart if he saw him.

"Stand down," he forced out. "Kaytlyn knows what she's doing."

"Okay, sir. The guy seemed like he really cared about her."

Cameron felt like his jaw was going to break from clamping it so hard. He hung up instead of responding. Forcing himself back into the vehicle, he clenched the steering wheel with his hands, bowed his head, and prayed like he hadn't prayed in years—not since he'd been trapped in a cave in Afghanistan wondering who would come through the opening next.

Please protect her right now while I can't. Please help me trust Kaytlyn, trust in thee, and trust in thy plan. Tell Jacob this "being patient" nonsense is killing me. He could almost hear his friend and boss laughing. Jacob would tell him it would all work out and encourage him to give it time.

Cameron released his grip on the steering wheel and leaned his head back. While he was nowhere near calm, he did his best to trust in Kaytlyn and the good Lord. He'd rather take five well-trained men on his own than sit immobile while the woman he loved was with another man, but he kept praying and hoping he could get through this. He didn't know what else to do.

CHAPTER TEN

Kaytlyn made it inside the lodge and collapsed on a couch. She wasn't sure where to start looking for Trey. Would he be at the Strongs' house in the nearby canyon, staying here at the lodge, at church, out on a bike ride?

She saw the security guys take up unobtrusive positions, but the open main level of the lodge wasn't that busy. Someone would notice them if they were observant. She pulled her phone out of her purse and sent Trey a text. *I really need to talk to you.*

The door to the lodge opened. Trey walked in, along with his friend Gavin, a beautiful girl she thought might be Gavin's little sister, and a young boy.

"Trey!" She didn't mean for it to be a cry, but she was so relieved that he was here. She could get this over with and get back to Cameron. Would Cameron hold her and maybe kiss her for real if she was pretend engaged to Trey? She was afraid the answer would be no. His sense of honor was strong and they needed to play their parts well to beat Peter and Jessica, especially if they had moles in the household staff.

She stood and apprehensively made her way toward the group. She did not want to do this with Trey, but what other option did she have? She had to protect her baby.

"Kaytlyn." Trey started toward her, his eyes full of concern, but then he stopped and turned back to the beautiful lady that had to be Gavin's sister. "Are you okay if I see what I can do to help her?"

"Of course." The young lady's dark eyes were kind, but there was a spark of jealousy there.

Oh, shoot. Was Kaytlyn going to mess up something for Trey? She'd been focused on her messed-up life, but Trey had a life as well and she wanted him to have every happiness.

"We'll just head in," the girl said. "Do you want me to order for you?"

"Sure. Whatever the special is will be great. Thanks." He bent down and gave her a quick kiss. "I'll be right there."

She smiled shakily and raised a hand to Kaytlyn. Kaytlyn waved back at her and the group, wishing she had time to talk to Gavin and his mother, who had always been kind to her. They all walked into the restaurant, but Trey hurried her direction.

"Trey," she breathed out when he reached her, grateful for a friend. She gave him a quick hug and then grabbed his arm. Her eyes darted to the picture windows and the man who was waiting for her in that car. Why couldn't she run to him? "Is there somewhere private we can talk?" she heard herself say.

Trey nodded. He directed her toward an office, typed a code on a keypad, swung open the door, and gestured Kaytlyn inside. She turned to him as soon as the door shut.

"Oh, Trey, I'm in a mess." The words just rushed out. Trey was a good man and she could trust him.

"What's going on?"

Trey's concern was comforting, but she wanted to be with Cameron and only Cameron, hang the stupid lawsuits. But what if Jessica could really take all the money that was being used to help people and, even more terrifying, take her child? Doing a fake fiancé for a short time was no big deal, yet emotion and the fear of losing her baby overwhelmed her. She sank down into a chair, buried her face in her hands, and started sobbing. She couldn't believe how weepy she'd felt since the day Jacob left them. She'd tried valiantly to bottle in too much emotion, and it all poured out at once.

Trey squatted next to her chair and touched her shoulder, probably wondering what had happened to his friend. "Kayt?"

She peered up at him through gritty eyes. Embarrassment rushed in. Poor Trey had no idea what hailstorm she was getting him into. "I'm sorry. I'm such a mess, and we drove to get here. Probably should've taken the plane, but I didn't want to wait on the pilot." She waved a hand. "I'm sure it's just pregnancy hormones."

Trey reared back. He pushed to his feet and then sank into the chair next to hers. "So you are ... pregnant?"

"Yes."

"Did you really suggest to Gavin that I might be the father?"

Now that she thought back on it, she realized it probably did sound that way. Oh, my. "Oh, Trey, I'm sorry. I'm so sorry. I don't want to involve you in any of this—I honestly want you to run away from me and never look back—but I don't know who to turn to." That wasn't true. She knew exactly who to turn to, but it was a bad idea. Jessica had all of those photos of her and Cameron during her marriage, making claims about them scheming to betray Jacob together. She lied and pretended she'd ever turn to her parents, "My parents can hardly handle the ranch, and Kandy's gone off the deep end, drugs, living on the street. You've always been such a good friend to me." Her lower lip trembled, and she concentrated on not breaking down into sobs again.

"Kayt ... I'll help you however I can, but I don't understand. Who is the father?"

She shook her head, fighting more tears. Trey was such a good person, but she didn't want to be with him, and his question brought back all the pain of Jessica's betrayal and now losing Jacob. "He's dead," she forced out. The actual father wasn't dead, but Jacob was, and it was easier than explaining the other nightmare with Peter.

A surge of all of her worries threatened to overwhelm her, but then—as if Jacob was watching out for her from above—the pain was washed away by resolve. She could handle all of it: Jessica's betrayal, the pregnancy, the sickness, hopefully becoming a single mom, running the businesses ... even staying away from Cameron.

"But I'm going to protect my baby, and I'm going to protect Jacob's legacy." It was her legacy too, really. Jacob had supported every idea she'd brought up, and together they'd done so much good for so many people. She couldn't lose sight of that now, and she couldn't allow Jessica and Peter to steal her child or ruin the future of her charitable foundation.

"What can I do to help you?"

Kaytlyn bit at her lip and stared at him, but then she shook her head. "Who were you with?" She tilted her head toward the lobby.

"Ella Strong." Trey smiled.

His happiness was contagious enough to make Kaytlyn smile too, and she thought of Cameron. "Do you ... care for her?"

"I love her."

Kaytlyn stood quickly. This was done. Thank heavens. "That's great, Trey. I'm so happy for you." She rushed to the door, flung it open, and hurried from the office. All she wanted was to get back to Cameron. But if they couldn't be fake engaged, how could they make this work and still protect the baby and everything she and Jacob had worked so hard for? She didn't know, but she wanted Cameron, right now.

Kaytlyn heard Trey's footsteps pursuing her, but she didn't stop. She ran to the Porsche and stopped next to the passenger door. As she looked in the driver's side window, she met

Cameron's gaze. His blue eyes were so full of love and devotion that she wanted to jump in, tell him to drive until they were alone, and then kiss him until everything somehow worked itself out.

"Kayt?" Trey called.

Her shoulders were trembling as she whirled to face him. She backed toward the vehicle, pressing against it for support and willing Cameron to jump out and come hold her. "I'm fine, Trey. I'm not burdening you with this."

She heard Cameron's door open, and then he was there. He stood between them with a fierce expression in his bright eyes, going chest to chest with Trey. She needed to tell him Trey wasn't the problem, but she loved that he'd come for her, as he always did.

"Mrs. Tarbet?" Cameron said. He was asking her how he should proceed, which she appreciated, but calling her Mrs. Tarbet? How weird was that? Was he trying to remind her of Jacob, or trying to keep his distance from her? Either way, she hated it.

"I'm fine, Cameron," she snapped. She wanted him to hold her and kiss her. "You don't call me Mrs. Tarbet."

"You're married?" Trey asked. "Wasn't Tarbet your boss's name?"

She nodded shortly. "Please wait in the car for me," she said to Cameron, knowing he'd obey. She really just wanted to end this conversation with Trey and get Cameron alone.

Cameron looked like he wanted to argue, but he simply said to Trey, "Hurt her and I'll cut your hands off."

Kaytlyn almost smiled at the threat. Cameron would always protect her, even if he didn't like his role in the situation.

Trey arched his eyebrows. "Thanks for the warning."

Cameron sent him a threatening look before meeting her gaze and instantly softening. The tenderness and love from this ultra-tough man stole her breath away. He quickly averted his gaze as if he knew he'd revealed too much, then stalked around to the driver's side and climbed in.

"Sorry." Kaytlyn folded her arms across her chest. "Cameron is my ... protection." The love of her life, the man she wanted to pledge everything to. She guessed protection would have to do as a descriptor for now.

"From who?" Trey's brow furrowed.

"I can't talk about it."

Trey stepped in closer. "Kayt. Let me help you. You're in a mess."

She shook her head but wrapped her arms around him, hugging him goodbye. They could never go back to the easy friendship they'd known for so many years. Trey held her close, relaying his strength to her. She wished it was Cameron holding her; this hug felt nothing like Cameron's touch. She stood on tiptoes and kissed Trey on the cheek, a bit closer to his lips than she'd intended. She fell back onto her heels, gave him one more fierce hug and said, "Thanks for being there for me."

"You won't even let me help you."

"It's okay." She was filled with determination. "I've got Cameron, and I'm not backing down to them. I'll be all right."

"You don't seem all right."

Kaytlyn sniffled and touched the back of her dripping nose with her fingertip. "I probably don't. It's just all so recent. Jacob passed a few days ago, and at the funeral, his daughter found out we were married and I was expecting his baby." She blew out a breath, deciding not to explain that she'd been the one to share the truth with Jessica and Peter and that it wasn't truly Jacob's baby. "It was an explosion. Our lawyer said if I'm engaged to someone great, it will help with the legal battle." If only she could be engaged to Cameron.

She didn't dare look in the car and forced a smile at Trey. "So I thought if you and I could do a fake fiancé to ..." She put a hand over her abdomen. "Protect my little man and my foundation from that evil, it would be good. But I can see you need to be with Ella." She pushed at his arm. "Go. Be with her."

"You wanted me to pretend to be engaged to you? For legal reasons?"

She nodded. "It's a big mess, Trey, and I'm not pulling you into it, especially if you are with Ella. Whatever you hear about me, please don't believe it." She smiled. "It was great to see you. I hope you'll be very happy." With that she opened the car door, slid in, and shut it firmly.

Looking over at Cameron, she saw his jaw was clenched so tightly that she could see a muscle twitching.

"Let's go," she muttered.

"Gladly." He started the car and sped away. His hands were

clenching the steering wheel so harshly, that his knuckles were turning white.

Kaytlyn wished she knew what to say to him, but her life just seemed to keep getting harder and messier. She couldn't even express how grateful she was to Cameron, but even upset like he was, he was her rock and she'd be lost without him. She had to concentrate on getting thorugh this fake fiancé ploy and the legal battle. Some day it would be her and Cameron's turn. Sadly not today.

CHAPTER ELEVEN

The other sport utility caught up with them after a couple of miles and fell in behind them as they drove through the valley. It was gorgeous today. Labor Day weekend. The Sabbath Day. How long had it been since Kaytlyn gone to church? Time had lost meaning with the pregnancy, sickness, and then losing Jacob. Her father would say she was going straight to Lucifer, but she was certain the Lord was a whole lot more merciful and understanding than that.

Silent minutes ticked by, and before she knew it, they were in the mountain pass headed out of the valley. She hadn't even enjoyed being home. Not that Colorado was really home anymore, but she'd always loved a lot of the people in her hometown.

"So ..." Cameron finally muttered.

"Trey's not going to work. He's in love."

"Good for him." Cameron sounded more relieved than if she'd just told him Jessica and Peter had driven off a cliff.

Kaytlyn laughed shortly. "It is good for him, but not good for proving that I'm 'stable.'" She didn't let herself look at Cameron. Here she was, figuring out how to make a stupid fake engagement work to prove she was in a stable relationship. She only wanted a relationship with the man next to her, but Larry had been more than adamant that it wouldn't in their favor. She could seek other legal counsel, but that would require trusting someone she didn't know with all of this mess, and she wasn't ready to do that. Jacob had trusted Larry implicitly, and she knew that Larry was doing everything he could for her. If it was only about the money, she'd walk away from it all for Cameron, but it was about more than that. She had to look out for the little one growing within her, along with her foundation and so many small businesses that Jessica and Peter would happily destroy, and she had a chance to prevent the evil Peter could accomplish in public office.

Pushing out a small breath, she muttered, mostly to herself, "There has to be someone else that would work." Dating wise, she'd been pretty reclusive for the past ten years, mostly working hard with Jacob. "Maybe we should turn around and I could talk to Gavin Strong. He's an awesome guy—smart, good-looking, trustworthy, and really stable."

"No," Cameron barked out.

She didn't look at him. If she did, she'd fold and tell him how much she loved him and how she could never be with someone else, no matter how fake it was. Instead, she kept chattering about the stupid fake fiancé idea to fill the stony silence in the car. "I don't know who else, Cam. Maybe one of the security guys? Or Richard Honeymiller? You know, the guy who helps me with the foundation? He's a great guy, and that would be a good fit. More believable because we have spent a lot of time togeth—"

"No!" Cameron roared.

She let herself look at him then. His blue eyes flashed, and he looked so angry that she was almost afraid of him. Almost. She knew Cameron too well to ever be afraid of him, no matter how tough he looked. This larger-than-life man brought her toast and tea every morning. She knew he was gentle and good through and through.

He turned off a side road in the canyon. Dust billowed around the vehicle as he sped along the rutted dirt road to a parking lot. It was the trailhead for a hike she'd gone on several times as a teenager. Cameron couldn't know that; he'd just pulled off at the first spot he could. Slamming the vehicle into gear, he jumped out and rushed around to her door. He flung it open, but before he could say anything, the other security guys were leaping out of their vehicle.

"Stay back," Cameron ordered.

They all paused in their tracks.

"Stay in the vehicle until I call for you." He was every inch their leader, and the three men obediently nodded and climbed back into the Porsche.

Kaytlyn stared up at Cameron. He was so strong, so in control.

She adored him, but she didn't want to cross him at the moment. "Did I say something wrong?" she asked quietly.

Cameron let out a half laugh, half grunt of frustration. Shaking his head, he slid his hands under her legs and behind her back, lifted her from the seat, and cradled her gently against his chest.

"Cam?" she whispered. Her stomach swooped in a good way at the joy of being held close to him and the determination and desire in his blue eyes.

"We're going to talk ... alone," he said.

Turning, he slammed the door with his hip and then strode up the trail with her in his arms. Kaytlyn wrapped her arms tightly around his neck and cuddled into his chest. She never wanted to leave this exact spot. If only she could forget about her responsibilities with the foundation and the businesses and the two of them could just escape. They could go to Jamaica and live out their lives with the baby in a remote village. His ten million was plenty of money.

They reached a clearing in the trees, far enough away from the parking lot that the men couldn't possibly hear or see them. Cam stopped and looked down at her. He gently set her on her feet but kept her in the circle of his arms.

"You okay?" she asked.

"No," he said shortly. He released her, and she swayed, missing his touch and wishing he would've kissed her instead of stepping away.

He paced a few steps, then rounded on her. "No, I am not okay. I am *done*, Kayt. Done listening to you talk about any other man, done leaving you alone with any other man, done even hearing about any other man." He looked so strong and handsome that it was all she could do to not rush at him. "You are *not* getting fake engaged to anyone else. You are *not* hugging anyone else *or* kissing them on the cheek."

Kaytlyn arched her eyebrows. Apparently, he'd seen her kiss Trey. It had been a goodbye kiss of friendship, but Cameron wouldn't want to hear that right now.

"I am *done*," he growled. "Do you hear me?"

Kaytlyn almost smiled, but this was no teasing moment. She wished she could put into words what his fierce protectiveness did for her. "Yes, Cam."

He stormed up to her, getting right in her space and wrapping his hands around her hips. "You are mine, Kayt. No one else's, never again. I want you. I need you. Please ..." His voice broke, and he cleared his throat before begging, "Please say you're mine."

Kaytlyn blinked up at him, willing the tears away. He was everything she'd always wanted: patient enough to nurse her while she was sick, strong enough to protect her from any threat, and brave enough to stand by her side no matter what. "Yes, Cam. I'm yours, completely yours."

He let out a soft groan and murmured, "I'm done being strong." Then he pulled her flush against him and kissed her. Kaytlyn responded to the devotion and passion in his lips, wrapping her arms tight around his broad back and kissing him back with all the desire that she'd been holding back for far too long.

The kisses took on a life of their own, and Kaytlyn loved each moment of his strong embrace, his lips claiming hers, and the warmth of his breath and their bodies intermingling. She loved him. Was it finally time to tell him that? What would happen when they got back to reality?

She pushed those worries away and kept up with the pace of his urgent kisses. Cameron was unreal, and his kisses branded her his as surely as the words they'd just said and the steady beating of her heart. She loved him. She wanted to shout it to the world.

When the kisses finally slowed down, because she could hardly catch a breath, Cameron rested his forehead against hers, cradling her more gently against him. "Did I hurt you?" he asked softly.

"Hurt me?" she asked in disbelief. "I'm not some delicate flower."

Cameron smiled and tenderly cupped her jaw. "I know, but you've been so sick, and there's the baby to think of."

"Thank you for being so sweet with me." She met his gaze, trying to convey her adoration and gratitude for him, but she also wanted him to know that she was strong. "Women, and babies, are tougher than that. You're not going to hurt me or the baby by kissing me passionately."

He let out a breath of relief. "Oh, thank the good Lord. I've been waiting for so long and I just—"

She stood onto tiptoes, pressing herself against him and kissing him long and hard. Pulling back, she asked playfully. "You just what?"

Cameron grinned. "I just ... completely lost my train of thought."

"Good."

Cameron swept her off her feet, kissing her as if the sun wouldn't come up tomorrow. Without him, it might not. Kaytlyn relished each kiss, each touch, and she didn't want her feet to touch the ground again.

Eventually, he did set her on the ground and simply held her close. "I feel like I've been waiting my whole life for you," he said softly.

"I'm worth the wait," she sassed.

Cameron chuckled. "Yes, you are." His blue eyes turned serious, and he tenderly kissed one cheek and then the other. "I love you so much, Kayt."

Her heart melted. Apparently, this was the right time to share how much she loved him.

"I never thought I'd feel like this again," he said.

Again? Kaytlyn perked up. She knew Cameron so well, yet in some areas she knew very little about him.

"After I lost Lori, I didn't think I'd ever love again."

"Lori?"

"We dated in college at UCLA and fell in love, but she was killed in a car rollover." He held her less tightly as his thoughts traveled back to the past. "I kind of shut myself off from relationships and love, but there was really no way to keep from falling for you." He smiled down at her. "You're amazing, Kayt. I've never been so impressed with anyone, so enthralled, so devoted."

Kaytlyn was grateful he'd shared this with her, and now she loved that she could tease him. "It's getting a bit deep."

He chuckled. "I know. My Army buddies would be rolling on the ground laughing if they could hear me now." He arched an eyebrow. "Especially if they could see inside my mind how desperately I've wanted you, how torturous it's been holding myself in check."

She framed his face with her hands. "You're an impressive man, Cameron Bodily, and I am completely in love with you."

He smiled, and she could see that he felt her words deeply.

"And as my irresistibly handsome man just told me, he was *done* —" She grinned as she emphasized the word just like he had. "— doing anything but kissing me night and day."

Cameron cocked an eyebrow. "I didn't know it came out quite like that, but I like it." He pulled her in close and kissed her, softly at first, but then the passion grew.

They were both completely invested in the kiss when footsteps and then a throat clearing drew them apart.

Cameron looked at Tyler, then back at her. "You're still the boss," he said to her. "Do I kill him for disobedience and interrupting that kiss, or just maim him?"

Kaytlyn laughed. "You're quite good at throwing around threats."

He arched an eyebrow and smiled slightly, and she could imagine that he'd follow through on any of those threats if it meant protecting her.

"I'm sorry, sir," Tyler said. "But the lawyer guy said he's been calling you two, and you're not answering, so he called me."

Kaytlyn's body deflated, and she sagged against Cameron. The real world come calling already. What would Larry say about Cameron's declaration that she wasn't doing a fake fiancé with anyone else? She knew he wouldn't like it, but he'd just have to tell Cameron no. She bit her lip to hide her smile, loving Cameron's determination.

Cameron nodded to Tyler. "We must be out of service up here. We'll come back down and call him."

"Thank you, sir." Tyler was always smiling, but he seemed to be hiding an extra-big smirk right now.

Cameron kept one arm around her back as they walked behind Tyler down the trail. He bent down close and his warm breath brushed her ear. "I'm not even close to being done kissing you, so be ready."

Kaytlyn's entire body filled with heat as she stared into his blue eyes. "I'll plan on it."

He winked at her.

They reached the parking lot, and Cameron pulled out his phone. "I still don't have service."

Kaytlyn's phone was in the Porsche. Cameron opened the door for her, and she retrieved it. Four missed calls from Larry. She held it up, and Cameron's brow furrowed.

Tyler climbed back into the Porsche to give them some privacy as Kaytlyn pushed the call back and speaker buttons. Cameron was obviously agitated, worrying about this call just like she was, but he didn't fidget; he got rigid and all military-looking. She hoped that kiss was not a one and done. She craved much, much more of Cameron and his amazing kisses.

The call connected, and Larry's voice came through the line. "Kaytlyn. How's it going with the ... fake guy?"

Kaytlyn studied Cameron, and he nodded encouragingly to her. "Um, not so good," she said. "He's already in a relationship."

Larry pushed out a heavy breath. "I've been trying to call you because I spoke privately with the judge who'll be mediating the cases."

Kaytlyn's heart started racing. "And?"

"She's not happy with the drama Jessica is creating, but Jessica and Peter are firmly entrenched in the political scene and have powerful allies. My friend warned me everything will have to be in place for you to win, especially with the baby, and nobody to cry foul and take it to the next level of courts."

Kaytlyn hadn't even thought of that. Even if they won, Jessica and Peter could appeal to another court. Would this ever end? Her shoulders felt heavy and she wanted to sink to the ground. Cameron's strong arm came around her waist, and she melted against him. No, she wanted to sink into his arms.

"Who else can you think of to do the fiancé gig?" Larry asked.

"Nobody," Cameron growled into the phone. "It's not happening."

"We have to make it happen, Cameron," Larry said, somewhat patiently. "Everything has to be in place."

Cameron's brow furrowed. "Then I'll do it." He smiled at Kaytlyn over the phone. "Happily."

Kaytlyn returned his smile, and a warm shiver ran through her at the promise of much more kissing to come. An engagement with Cameron would not be fake at all. Not to her.

"No," Larry broke into their moment and wiped the smiles from both of their faces. "I've already explained why that won't work." Cameron opened his mouth to argue, but Larry cut him off. "You're not a selfish man, Cameron. Don't start acting like one at this crucial time."

Cameron's mouth clamped shut and that muscle worked in his jaw. How she wanted to kiss that muscle, kiss that jaw, kiss that mouth.

"Larry," Kaytlyn protested. "There is nothing selfish about this. I love Cameron and don't want to be with anyone else."

Cameron gave her half of a smile, but she could see that Larry's comment about selfishness had stung.

A heavy silence followed. Then Larry said, "I thought you were both committed to protecting Jacob's legacy, the foundation, and especially, the baby. I thought you were both committed to keeping all that you and he worked so unselfishly to build from Peter and Jessica, who will be all too thrilled to destroy it."

He paused, and the quiet was broken only by the birds chirping and a rustle of the wind in the leaves. Kaytlyn clung to the phone and tried to catch Cameron's eye, but he was studying the phone.

"Was I wrong?" Larry's voice came through, clear and direct.

It hurt deep inside. Kaytlyn hadn't felt the awful sickness in days, but the thought of losing her baby, and everything Jacob had worked a lifetime for—simply because she couldn't resist being with Cameron any longer,—was like a sword piercing straight through her.

Cameron's blue eyes searched hers. Silent communication passed between them, and she knew they'd both do what they had to do. The stakes were too high. Yet the agony of not being Cameron's was as bad as imagining Jessica destroying Jacob's life work. She couldn't let herself think about if Jessica and Peter were awarded her baby, and sadly that was the more precarious case. Especially if they could prove she'd willingly signed those papers and was unstable and an unfit mother.

"You weren't wrong," Cameron said in an even voice that impressed and terrified Kaytlyn. Would he pull away from her completely? Would they revert back to the past twelve weeks of being so close, yet so far away?

"What do you think we should do?" Kaytlyn managed to ask.

"Find the perfect person for the fake fiancé," Larry said. "Someone you can trust who won't go flapping their mouth. You have to convince even the staff that you're with him, because you know Jessica has spies somewhere in the house. Find someone who looks good and stable. Someone who Cameron won't kill when the man touches you." The last sentence was said with a bit of humor, but neither of them laughed.

"We'll be in touch," Cameron said shortly. He took the phone from Kaytlyn's hand and ended the call. After a moment of deep thought, he walked away from Kaytlyn, set her phone in the console of the sport utility, then started pacing the parking lot.

Kaytlyn wanted to reach out to him, to tell him it would all work out. Larry had gotten a little more intense today, but she had to keep believing it would all be okay. She couldn't lose her baby. No matter what.

Finally, Cameron stopped and turned to face her. His broad shoulders were rounded, and she'd never seen such a defeated look on his face. "Are you all right?" he asked.

Kaytlyn didn't know why she was surprised. Everything he did was for her. She'd loved Jacob like a best friend or a brother, but she'd never had a man she could love and trust in every possible way like she did Cameron. She nodded. "We'll get through this, Cam."

His eyes traced over her face. He gently cupped her cheek with his hand and placed a chaste kiss on her lips. "Hopefully it won't last too long."

"For sure."

"Will you pray for me, Kayt?"

"I always do."

He smiled at that.

"Anything specific I need to pray for? Besides you not killing whoever does the fake fiancé role?"

He smiled wryly at that. "Definitely pray for that. And pray I can be unselfish and put you, the baby, and Jacob's legacy before my own wants and desires."

"Ah, Cam." She flung her arms around his neck and pulled herself up close to him, hugging him fiercely. "You're the most unselfish person I know."

"I feel like the most selfish one. If you just knew how irresistible you are, how much I love you, you'd see how hard this is for me."

"I think I can understand, because I literally crave you more than sleep, food ... anything in this world."

Cameron let out a soft groan and captured her lips with his own. The kiss was powerful but short. He pulled back, and his eyes roved over her face as if memorizing every detail. He said in a low voice, "This is going to have to sustain me for a while."

She wished she could say he was being silly to think they couldn't kiss. A fake engagement would be no big deal. She loved Cameron and no one else, but she also loved how honorable he was. She knew he would be hands-off, not only because anyone catching them could mess up the entire ploy, but because he honored commitments—fake or not.

He released her from the hug. Taking her hand, he walked toward the other vehicle. The three men inside were studying the trees, obviously not wanting to get caught watching their boss's kiss.

Opening the driver door, Cameron said, "Tyler, we need you."

Tyler popped out of the car and bounced from foot to foot. He wasn't usually a nervous guy, but his typical smile was only partially there. "Everything okay, sir?"

Tyler had been hired at the recommendation of Sutton Smith. He'd come straight out of West Point. He didn't have the military experience Cameron or some of the others did, but he had a stable family he went to visit often in Georgia, and he was a great guy, if a little young for her. She found that a little funny. She'd been married to a man thirty years her senior; now she would possibly be engaged to one five years younger.

"We need your help," Cam said.

"Anything, sir."

Cam nodded. "You're a good man." He squeezed Kaytlyn's hand and pushed out a heavy breath. "We need to do a very temporary arrangement. Very."

Kaytlyn hoped it was temporary, but she was worried. Waiting on court dates and appeals could take years. She clung to Cameron's hand. She didn't want to pretend to be with another man, no matter how nice and smiley he was.

"What do you need?" Tyler appeared eager to please. He was a good-looking guy with dark hair and a trimmed beard and that ready smile, but the thought of even holding his hand made her stomach squirm. At least when she'd contemplated this with Trey, she knew him well and was comfortable with him.

"We need you to fake an engagement with Kayt."

Tyler reared back. "Excuse me?"

"I know this is unconventional, but we'll give you a large bonus at the end of the agreement, say ..." Cameron glanced at Kaytlyn.

"A hundred and fifty thousand," she said. She could easily go higher, but that was more than Tyler made in a year, so it would be a good bonus.

Tyler's eyes bugged out.

"I'll talk to the other security guys and explain what's going on, but no one else can know. No one," Cameron explained.

"But ... why?"

"It's a long story, but you remember Jacob's daughter from the funeral?"

"Yeah, wish I didn't."

"If she and her husband win the lawsuits against Kayt, they'll take everything Jacob and Kayt have worked so hard for. They're even trying to get the baby."

Tyler's gaze dropped to Kaytlyn's abdomen, then back to her face. "But faking we're engaged ...?"

"Helps to prove Kaytlyn's in a safe, stable relationship and the baby will have a good home."

Tyler looked at their joined hands. "Why can't you do it, sir?"

"Believe me, I have begged for the position." Cameron scrubbed at his face with his free hand. "But sadly, that would give Jessica more ammunition. I'm not the right one for the job. You are."

Kaytlyn couldn't believe this was happening. She didn't feel right about it, mostly because nothing but Cameron by her side felt right.

"So what would I need to do?" Tyler asked.

"Hopefully we can keep it pretty simple," Cameron said. "We'd take some pictures of you two ... together." He cleared his throat as if that was painful to say. "Leak them to the media, and it should spread pretty quick. I mean, Jacob hasn't been gone very long; people will love the speculation and drama of it. Maybe in public you'll have to stay close to Kayt, pretend you're ... together. At home, in the front of the staff, I guess you'd have to pretend as well to be ... together."

Kaytlyn would've laughed at how hard Cameron was struggling to lump her together with anyone else, but she knew exactly how he felt.

"How long do you think?"

Cameron shrugged. "I don't know. Our lawyer is working hard, and we're hopeful the lawsuits will wrap up before Christmas."

"So hopefully just a few months?"

"Yeah."

"I'll do it."

Cameron forced a smile at him. "Thanks, man. When I knew we had to do this, I wanted someone I could trust, someone I respect. That's why I picked you."

"Thank you, sir." Tyler beamed like he'd been given an honor.

Cameron nodded, but then his voice became louder and stronger. "And if you look at or touch Kayt inappropriately, I will slit your throat."

Kaytlyn shook her head. Cameron and his threats. Yet she secretly loved his intensity.

Tyler gulped. "Yes, sir."

Cameron looked back at her. "Here's to getting through the next few months without me slitting his throat."

Kaytlyn laughed. She couldn't help it. Cameron laughed with her, though it was obviously strained. Tyler gave a nervous chuckle, but he understandably didn't think it was funny, as it was his throat that might be slit.

Her laughter faded away as she contemplated. Three more months without kissing Cameron. He had impressive self-control, but she wasn't quite sure how she would survive. She would have thought those kisses could sustain her, but they already just left her wanting more.

Cameron gave her a grim smile, and her heart leapt for him. Three more months. She was going to have to pray hard, and maybe somehow she'd make it through.

CHAPTER TWELVE

After they made the agreement, Cameron forced himself to position Kaytlyn and Tyler so it looked like they were holding hands or staring into each other's eyes in the very trees where he'd given her the kisses to end all kisses. He dreamt about those kisses almost every night.

Kaytlyn had sent the pictures to some trusted media sites, saying that while she didn't want to hide anything, she'd grown to trust and love one of her security personnel through the long months of Jacob's illness. Cameron liked that at least that part was true. The pictures had exploded online with all kinds of speculation about Kaytlyn, Jacob's foundation and companies that were now in her name, the lawsuits that had been made public from Jessica's and Peter's lawyer, the baby she was expecting, and of course when or if she would marry her new man.

Two and a half miserable months passed, and around Thanksgiving time, they put a diamond ring on Kaytlyn's finger and sent around more pictures of the newly engaged couple. The media was surprisingly supportive and kind to Kaytlyn. Cameron thought it was because she was so angelic that no one could hate her—except for Jessica and Peter.

Luckily, they were pretty reclusive and rarely left the mansion, so they could stage most of the time that Kaytlyn had to be close to Tyler. Cameron kept track of her through cameras, watching as she worked long hours, took her meals alone, and slept more than usual. He wondered if she was worn out from the pregnancy and all she was trying to accomplish before the baby came, or if she was as depressed as he was.

Cameron missed her. It was an awful ache that felt like an elephant sitting on his chest. He'd forced himself to rearrange the schedule so he wasn't her direct guardian. He couldn't stand to love her like he did and be close; any fool would notice a touch or a longing look between them. To do this stupid fake fiancé right, he'd realized he'd have to keep his distance, because he didn't want to slit Tyler's throat, not really. Okay, maybe occasionally, when he saw them holding hands.

Luckily, there'd been no signs of physical threats from Jessica or Peter. They seemed to be keeping busy with life, waiting on the lawsuits to come to fruition. They had a court date of December third. The judge, luckily the same one Larry had spoken with, hadn't been reassigned, and would rule on all counts that day. The end was in sight. Cameron prayed it was a good end. He knew Jessica and Peter wouldn't go down easily, but he thought it was mostly about the money for them. Protecting Kaytlyn's child was much more important to him, and would probably be the tougher battle with those papers she'd signed.

He tried to think positive thoughts. He'd assigned Tyler to stay by Kaytlyn's side as much as possible. They tried to act like they were flirting or talking around the staff, and it made Cameron's stomach tie up in knots. He got through the days a little easier when he focused on monitoring security for the rest of the property, training and working with the security guys who were off duty, and exercising extra hours to burn off the frustration—lots of extra hours.

He hadn't moved his rooms, though, and he was still sleeping in the suite next to Kaytlyn's. It soothed him somehow to know she was close, even if he wouldn't let himself do anything about it. Sometimes that struck him as so idiotic. Why couldn't he sneak into her room to hold and kiss her? No one would know.

He leaned back in bed and shook his head. He and the good Lord and Jacob would know. Kaytlyn was engaged, and they were both focused on protecting the foundation and the baby and Jacob's legacy. Someday soon, the timing would be right. He just wished it would be really soon.

He drifted off to sleep, dreaming of those kisses in that meadow in Colorado.

A strangled scream woke him. His vision was blurry as he leapt out of bed and hurtled himself toward the door. Kaytlyn!

Dodging to the next door over, he burst into her room. "Kayt!" he called urgently.

He heard a whimper. His eyes were still gritty, but he could see, and as they adjusted to the dimly lit room, he could tell she was still in bed. Keeping one eye on her, he hurriedly checked the rest of the suite, the bathroom, and the closet. There were no other threats. Was she having a nightmare?

Easing close to her bedside, he let himself look at her as she slept. She was absolutely gorgeous in a white tank top with her long blond hair tousled, and the white bedding reminded him of how close to an angel she was. As he stared at her, his thoughts were nowhere close to angelic, and he forced himself to slowly back away, though every male instinct was saying to sit on the edge of the bed and cradle her in his arms.

Her face twisted in fear and then she cried out, "No!"

Cameron startled. He stepped closer. Should he wake her?

"Please," she whimpered, twisting in the sheets. The outline of her baby bump was revealed, another curve that he loved about her. Thinking about the baby itself still felt surreal, but he kept hoping he could be the little one's father.

Cameron let himself sit on the edge of the bed like he knew he shouldn't. He reached out to gently touch her arm. The smooth skin under his palm was so appealing, so irresistible. He found himself leaning even closer and placing both of his hands on each of her upper arms.

"Help!" she suddenly shrieked. "Cam!" The wail of his name pierced through him.

Cameron wrapped his hands around her shoulders. "Kayt, Kayt! Wake up!"

Her head thrashed and she was back to whimpering, "No, no, no, Cam!"

"Kayt! You're having a nightmare. Wake up." He lifted her up off the pillow, sliding his hands behind her back and her body against his chest. "Kayt, it's me, it's Cam. Wake up!"

Her eyes flew open and she stared up at him. "Cam?" she whispered.

He let out a breath of relief. "Yes, it's Cam. You're okay. It was just a nightmare." But his heart was thumping wildly. He wasn't sure if it was from the concern for her and what must've been a horrible nightmare, or if it was simply his body's reaction to having her in his arms again.

"Oh, Cam. Thank you." She leaned into him, her arms coming around his back to cling to him and her head fitting in the crook of his neck like it was designed for her.

"What was it, love?" he asked, wincing as soon as the words left his mouth. He didn't want to make their separation harder on her. For over two months, they hadn't touched or kissed, and now he was right back on the verge of declaring his unending devotion.

"You ... Peter hired some men to torture and kill you and made me watch." Her eyes traced over him. "But you're here. You're okay. He won't hurt you."

He smiled. "I'm here, Kayt. No one's going to hurt me, and I'll always be here for you."

She stared at him, her blue eyes uncertain and vulnerable. "Will you?"

"Of course."

"Then be there for this." She pulled herself up and kissed him.

The kiss was fierce, needy, and incredible. Cameron heard some very quiet voices in his head telling him to stop, but he had no such inclination. He wrapped his arms around her waist, lifted her up against the headboard, and leaned in, kissing her with all the passion he'd been storing up the past two months. He'd ached for her, and right now he was going to show her exactly how much he'd missed her.

K aytlyn felt the incredible warmth and pressure of Cameron's mouth coming down hard on hers and his upper body pressing her into the headboard. She held on tightly to his muscular back and continued to receive and give kiss after kiss. She loved him, and she'd missed him so horribly these past two months. She knew he'd kept his distance so they could accomplish the fake fiancé ploy with Tyler, but she'd hated every single second without him.

Forcing that from her mind, she happily concentrated on his mouth, righting the wrongs of the time they'd had to be apart. His lips were firm, demanding, yet somehow tender. She knew Cameron would always have her best interests in mind, and he understood that right now, her best interests lay in his thorough and wonderful kisses.

When he finally drew back, they were both breathing heavily. Kaytlyn was ready to take some deep breaths and move in for round two.

Cameron's hands came to her face and he cradled her jaw, staring deeply at her. "Ah, Kayt," he murmured. "I've missed you. I can't even tell you how much—"

Kaytlyn wrapped her arms around his biceps and kissed him in response, trying to show him through her kiss how much she'd missed him. Only a couple more weeks until the case was hopefully over, and then she would be done with the farce of her engagement. She was going to propose to this man, and they were going to fly to a tropical island and be married immediately. The thought brought a warm flush, and she clung tighter to him and deepened the kiss.

Cameron did the last thing she'd imagined he would do: he broke the kiss and leaned back. Staring at her with eyes full of desire and need, he shook his head firmly. "We can't, Kayt. Soon this will all be over. Right now, I need to keep my distance."

With those awful words, he pulled away from her and stood next to the bed.

Kaytlyn felt bereft, dejected, and angry. She stood right next to him and wrapped her arms around his strong back, laying her head against his warm chest. She absolutely loved when he wasn't wearing a shirt. "Keep your distance?" she demanded. "Has anything ever felt this incredible, this right to you?"

Cameron let out a groan and wrapped his arms around her, holding her tight and making her heart leap. He wouldn't push her away. He loved her too much.

"No, Kayt," he whispered, tenderly kissing her forehead. "Nothing ever has."

She looked up at him. Her eyes stung with tears of relief, joy, and the pain of the past two months—no, the past five months—but everything was right when she was here in his arms.

His eyes swept carefully over her face. "But that doesn't mean this is right."

Kaytlyn's stomach dropped.

"We're almost there, love. We've both been so strong, waited so long. Two more weeks and the court will rule. Either way, we'll deal with their ruling, even if it means I take you away to some deserted island where Peter and Kaytlyn will never touch your baby. Either way, we can be together. It'll be that much sweeter because of our wait."

Kaytlyn blinked away the moisture in her eyes. Cameron loved her so much he'd run with her to protect the baby. She loved him back and tried to be strong like he was. "As soon as it's over, we're flying to Aruba and being married on the beach."

He let out another groan and gave her one quick, tender kiss. "We'll have a Christmas wedding."

"Christmas?" She shook her head. "I'm talking December fourth."

Cameron chuckled. "I like the way you think."

"You just like me."

"Yes, I definitely do, but I've got to get out of here before I start thinking about being married to you."

Kaytlyn drew in a deep breath, knowing exactly how hard this was for him. She forced herself to release her grip on him and step back.

Cameron stared down at her, his blue eyes full of longing. "Two more weeks," he said. The promise in his words made her stomach flutter and her heart beat harder. "We can do this."

Kaytlyn nodded, forcing a brave smile. "Two more weeks," she repeated. "I love you."

"I love you too." He looked like he wanted to kiss and hold her again, but instead he spun on his heel and marched out of the room.

Kaytlyn watched his broad, muscular shoulders clear the door-frame. He looked so good, she wanted to run after him and just touch and kiss him one more time. Instead, she collapsed on her bed, burying her face in the pillow as the tears leaked out. Two more weeks. Could she make it two more weeks without him?

She turned onto her side and wrapped her hands around her small baby bump. She'd started feeling slight motions from within. She'd decided not to find out the sex, but in her heart, she knew it was a boy. She cradled the baby and let the tears run. "I promise to protect you and put you first." The baby was the only thing that could get her through and help her to be strong when all she wanted to do was run into the room next door, kiss that spectacular man, and forget every promise she'd ever made to anyone but him.

CHAPTER THIRTEEN

Cameron had another fabulous memory of kissing Kaytlyn, but now it would be even harder to keep his distance. He'd held everything in his arms, knew the incredible rush of kissing her and hoping for even more, and it had once again been ripped away from him by his own stupid self-declared mandate. Sometimes when he thought about that night, he let himself wonder what would have happened if he hadn't stopped kissing her. Then he had to hurry somewhere private, drop to his knees, and pray for help and forgiveness.

They got through Thanksgiving dinner. Kaytlyn looked incredibly beautiful next to Tyler at the large dining table. They sat down and ate with all the staff members who didn't have family close by. Kaytlyn talked and laughed with Tyler and those seated close to her, and she only gave Cameron a few longing glances. Cameron spent much of the meal studying the people at the table, and it was hard to imagine that any of them could betray Kaytlyn to Jessica.

The staff decorated the house in Christmas lights, greenery, and red and silver decorations. He lost track of how many Christmas trees and wreaths they had. Snow covered the valley, and icicles hung from rafters. Christmas cheer and warmth were spreading everywhere, but Cameron couldn't share it with the one person who would make it all mean something. He wished his heart was made of ice colder than the wind chill outside.

He'd started with the chant of two more weeks, but then it became ten more days, nine more days, eight more days. On day seven and counting, Larry texted them both to meet him in Kaytlyn's office immediately.

Cameron left the security center in the basement and climbed the stairs. Kaytlyn was descending the stairs from above. He stopped on the landing and just stared at her. Luckily, there weren't any household staff in the foyer at the moment, so he could drink in his fill of her beauty set against the greenery draping the thick wooden railings.

She saw him watching and smiled. "Fancy meeting you here."

"You look as beautiful as ever." He grinned, his heart thumping wildly. Could he just kiss her once today? Maybe once each day until the trial would sustain him. But no, he'd committed to showing she was engaged to Tyler, because there might be house staff who were still loyal to Jessica. He wanted it to look real, and he really wanted to get through it.

She reached the bottom step and put a hand over her abdomen. Her pale blue sweater hugged her curves perfectly, and when she paired it with fitted jeans and high heels, she looked classy and irresistible. They stood only ten feet apart, but it might as well have been a mile for all the good it did him. Yet Cameron still felt close to her emotionally. These battles they'd been through, against Jessica and against their own desires, had made them stronger and more in love. Now if he could only last seven more days.

The doorbell rang, and Kaytlyn jumped. "Oh!" It was so cute how it surprised her and how invested she'd been in him.

Beau, one of his security guys, hurried into the foyer but stopped when he saw the two of them. "Oh. Hey, boss."

"I'll get the door," Cameron told him. "It's for us."

"Thank you." Beau tilted his chin up and left again, back to monitoring the property from the security rooms in the basement. Cameron loved this sprawling mansion and the staff had a familial feel, but when he and Kaytlyn got married and he knew she and the baby were safe from Jessica and Peter, he might talk to her about dismissing most of the staff or maybe even buying a small rambler, just for the two of them and their baby.

Cameron forced himself to stop staring at Kaytlyn and dreaming of being married to her. He turned to the door, checking his phone and the security cameras to make sure it really was Larry before swinging it wide.

Larry burst through the front door in a flurry of cold air and a huge smile. "Get in the office, get in the office," he demanded.

Cameron turned to Kaytlyn with an arched brow. "I think he means us."

Kaytlyn giggled so appealingly that Cameron wanted to kiss her. Wait, that was nothing new; Cameron always wanted to kiss her.

Larry rushed into the office and yanked his laptop and then a bunch of papers out of his shoulder bag. Cameron waited for Kaytlyn to cross the foyer. He shouldn't have done it, but he let himself put his hand on the small of her back. Contentment and desire rose quickly in him. Kaytlyn smiled sweetly up at him and murmured for only him to hear, "I've missed you horribly."

"Nowhere near as bad as I've missed you," he whispered back.

She bit at her lip and said, "Nope, I've got you beat. I've missed you, like, five hundred times as much."

Cameron was about ready to press her into the wall and show her exactly how much he'd missed her when Larry interrupted, "Come on, you two, get in here! This is amazing news!"

Cameron was skeptical. The only amazing news he wanted was that he could take her to that island and marry her. Today. He escorted her to her desk chair, and she sat down. He stood beside her and forced himself to look at Larry. The man was practically glowing with excitement.

"They asked for a settlement," Larry blurted out.

"Come again?" Cameron asked. They'd heard no indication that Jessica and Peter were even interested in a settlement.

Larry nodded. "Yes, it's incredible. Judge Peterson just called me. She met separately with them and their lawyer. They want fifty million for Peter's campaign and they want to look like the most benevolent people anybody has ever seen." He hooted, holding up the papers that must have been the settlement. "This is a dream come true."

"I don't care about the money." Kaytlyn stood quickly. "What about my baby?" She cradled her stomach.

Larry grinned happily. "That's where their fake benevolence comes in. They've signed away their rights to the baby."

Kaytlyn's breath popped out loud enough he could hear it. Her hands were trembling as she touched the papers Larry was holding. "We pay them fifty million and they drop all the lawsuits and charges?" Her voice dropped and had a catch in it. "They have no right to my baby ... ever?"

"Yes! Yes, Kaytlyn! Can you believe it?"

Kaytlyn let out a happy cry and clasped her hands together.

Cameron was ready to celebrate with them but something felt fishy. He'd wondered all along if it was only about the money and if they'd sign off on the baby for it, but why the fifty million that had set Jessica off that fateful night? She hadn't wanted Kaytlyn to have even fifty million of her inheritance money, or the foundation, and now she was willing to walk for that same amount?

"Do they have any clue what Jacob was worth?" The last number Cameron had seen was four point eight billion. Who just walked away from that with a fifty-million-dollar settlement? Especially if they were crazy enough to think they deserved it all like Jessica did. He highly doubted she was rational enough to worry that she wouldn't win.

"I know! But Peter's career is too important to him and think of the positive publicity they'll get for walking away and especially for giving Kaytlyn the baby. Imagine all the credit they will claim for allowing the foundation to continue, at great sacrifice to themselves. Honestly I don't care about their motivation, I've received all the paperwork." Larry shook the papers again. "I'll need you to sign and get me a check to hand to them. And it's done." He beamed. "You two have done it. You're finally free."

Cameron leaned into the chair that Kaytlyn had been sitting in. Free. Free to ... His strength returned in a rush, and he didn't care what Jessica's motivations were, only that they were free. He whipped to face Kaytlyn, and she threw herself against him. Cameron swept her off her feet, swinging her around as she laughed; then he set her down and proceeded to kiss her, showing her how horribly he'd missed her and promising they wouldn't be apart again.

"All right, you two, I need the signatures and the check."

Cameron reluctantly released her. "To be continued," he said in a low voice.

"That better be a promise," she shot back.

"Oh, it is."

K aytlyn could not believe their good luck. Fifty million might sound like a huge settlement, but it was nothing compared to the resources Jacob had bestowed upon her. To have Jessica and Peter give her the baby and walk away for so little was the golden ticket. No, having them walk away at all was more than she'd hoped.

Even more important to her, her baby was safe from their schemes and from legal battles. She was finally free to be with Cameron. They signed the papers and walked Larry to the front door with a check in hand. Kaytlyn's smile was so big it hurt her cheeks.

Cameron shut the door behind Larry and turned to her. The plan had worked, and now they could be together. He had an almost wicked gleam in his blue eyes as he approached her. "Finally," Cameron murmured. She was waiting for him to sweep her off her feet and kiss her, but instead he reached for her left hand and slid the engagement ring off of it. Then he took her hand and walked her into the office. Tossing the ring on the desk, he said, "We'll donate that to charity."

"Sounds good," she laughed, but the anticipation of him kissing her was crowding out everything else.

Cameron dropped onto one knee and reached for both of her hands. "Kayt ..." He smiled so tenderly. "I love you. Will you please put me out of my misery and marry me?"

She tilted her head as if considering it. "I'll think about it."

His eyes widened. "Kayt. Please. I can't stand being without you anymore."

Kaytlyn smiled and leaned down, giving him a soft kiss. "If you promise to elope, I'll marry you as soon as possible."

"Yes!" Cameron let out a roar that shocked her and made her laugh. He leapt to his feet and lifted her up above his head. "Yes!" Lowering her, he pulled her in tight and sealed the proposal with a lingering kiss. With his mouth still so close, she could feel the word as he breathed, "Today?"

Kaytlyn laughed. "How about tomorrow?"

Cameron groaned. "You need a dress, right? Oh, and we definitely need to go shopping for a ring."

She loved the idea of shopping with him, and she could hardly wait to wear his ring. "And I have a doctor's appointment at nine tomorrow morning. Probably should get his clearance before we leave for, where was it? Aruba?"

"Actually, I've been researching, and Grand Cayman has no waiting period." He pumped his eyebrows. "So I've been in contact with the Ritz-Carlton on Seven Mile Beach. The wedding planner and I are on pretty good terms."

"Are you serious?" Kaytlyn could not believe her tough, military man was on standby with a wedding planner.

"Yeah. Nessa has got everything ready from the suite for our honeymoon—" He smiled even more broadly. "—to the intimate wedding and dinner. Do you care if I invite my parents? I know that's not really eloping, but my mom has gone through so much with three deployments and me rarely making it home to visit. I'd love for them to be part of it."

Kaytlyn felt a pang. "Of course. I can't wait to meet them. Cam, we can wait longer than a day and invite anyone you want."

He shook his head. "I just want you. Maybe we'll let Tyler come as our security." He winked. "Make him feel some of the misery I've felt watching you sit by him and touch his hand."

"Oh, Cam." She hated that he had been in misery, but she had been as well. "I don't think it would be that hard on Tyler. He doesn't love me."

"He'd better not," Cameron growled. He pulled her in and gave her a very thorough kiss.

Kaytlyn's world was lit with joy as he manipulated her mouth with his. The way he'd said "finally" a few minutes ago rushed over her again. Finally, they were free to be together, without any strings, guilt, or worries.

He pulled back and his eyes slid over her. "No one could ever love you like I do."

"That is for sure."

He kissed her again, but then his eyes looked troubled as he said, "Wait. Who do you want at the wedding? We went to your hometown and didn't even go see your parents because I was so stirred up and frustrated. Kayt, I'm sorry. Let's fly there tomorrow after the doctor and shopping. Invite them to the wedding, or at the very least I need to get your father's permission." He shook his head. "I've waited so long and did all the research for the honeymoon, but I'm doing it all wrong. I don't even have your father's permission."

Kaytlyn felt a burst of nausea like the morning sickness was back, but that was silly; she was five months along now and hadn't had morning sickness in almost two. She tried not to think about the heartbreak of her family too often, but she wanted to steal her mom and youngest sister from her father's clutches. She looked down and admitted, "I don't know how they'll treat us, Cam."

"Your parents?"

She broke away and sat down in her office chair. "I told you the story of how Jacob found me at Perry's Restaurant ten years ago?"

"Yeah. On one of our hikes before you got sick."

She nodded, remembering. She'd really enjoyed those hikes and just talking with Cameron. It had been a hard time, because he'd obviously held himself back while she'd been married to Jacob, but she'd still loved getting to know him. "I didn't tell you about why I left home at eighteen and never went back."

"You told me you just wanted to escape the valley you'd grown up in."

"I actually loved Lonepeak Valley, but my dad was emotionally abusive and ultra-controlling. One of my sisters was driven to drugs and alcohol, the one in the pictures you saw. My younger sister and mom are like puppets and work night and day to try to keep my dad happy."

Cameron's eyes were wide. "Kayt. And look how amazing you turned out. I had no idea."

"Being close to Jacob is the only reason I have any confidence and ability."

"We owe Jacob a lot, but I think your confidence and ability is inherent."

"Thank you." She studied her hands for a second, then said, "Jacob and I tried to visit my parents and youngest sister a few years ago. My father was horrible, claimed Jacob and I were in a twisted relationship and said so many awful things. Jacob walked away." She gave him an appraising look. "I think you'd snap him in half."

"Hey." Cameron held his hands up. "I like to make threats and follow through with those threats when it's deserved, but I wouldn't go after your father because he called me names."

Kaytlyn swallowed. "What if he called me names?"

His eyebrows rose and his jaw got tight. "That I couldn't tolerate."

Lifting her hands, she said, "So I don't know that asking for my hand is the best idea."

"We'll send a nice card and a wedding picture."

Kaytlyn laughed in relief.

Cameron sat on the edge of the desk next to her and took her hand. "Maybe we should try, though. They are your parents, and I really would like to go about this the right way, get their blessing, invite them. If they choose to not want to be part of our lives, that's their loss."

Kaytlyn smiled up at him. He was amazing, and she was done worrying about how her parents would react. They'd deal with that tomorrow, and maybe she'd get the chance to ask Krysta to leave with her again. "So what do you want to do right now?" she asked. Their whole lives were in front of them, and she had some pretty good ideas of what she'd like to do now.

Cameron walked over to the office door and firmly shut it. As he returned to where she sat, his smile grew broader, and Kaytlyn loved seeing this carefree, happy side of him. He scooped her out of the chair, holding her against his chest; then he sat in the chair and grinned down at her. "So first I plan on kissing you for a long, long time."

"I guess I could tolerate that," she teased.

"Tolerate?" His eyebrows shot up, and then his blue eyes narrowed. "I'll have you begging for more."

Kaytlyn already was, but she didn't admit it. "I'll decide."

With a chuckle, he bent his head and took his time, almost teasing her with soft, light kisses, drawing back each time before she could extend the kiss and holding her so she couldn't get what she wanted.

Kaytlyn needed more, needed her warrior to take complete control. "If you're going to kiss me, kiss me," she demanded, panting for air.

"Begging?" he asked.

"Yes!"

Cameron grinned, and then he complied. His mouth came down on hers with all the passion and fire she knew he reserved only for her. She'd throw her pride out the window and beg for these kisses every day. Happiness filled her as she realized that now she could. Their fight was over, her baby was theirs, and they could kiss and hold each other all day long if they wanted to. Kaytlyn definitely, definitely wanted to.

CHAPTER FOURTEEN

Kaytlyn was groggy the next morning, as she and Cameron had stayed up late, holding each other close, kissing, talking, and dreaming. She hurried to deal with some fires with work, get ready for her doctor's appointment at nine a.m., and pack a bag. They were taking the jet and flying first to Colorado and then on to Grand Cayman, after they went shopping for a ring and a dress.

She was just zipping up her suitcase, with ten minutes to spare before they needed to leave, when there was a soft rap on her bedroom door. "Come in," she called from the closet.

Cameron walked in with a tray as she hurried into the bedroom from her closet, tugging the suitcase behind her. The tray had tea and toast on it.

She grinned. "I don't know if I'll be able to drink ginger tea again in my life."

He chuckled. "Well, lucky for you, this is raspberry leaf tea. Cathy said it helps with the pregnancy and is even good for labor."

"Well, I'm not even close to worrying about that."

He winked. "When it happens, I'll be right here holding your hand."

Kaytlyn glanced sharply at him. "Will you?"

Cameron set the tray down on a side table and stepped up closer to her. "Yes, I will," he said decisively. "I want to be in every part of this little one's life."

Kaytlyn sighed. "Have I told you that I love you?"

"Not today."

She smiled and eased in closer. "I love you, and I can't wait to be married to you. The little one and I want you in every part of our lives."

He wrapped his hands around her stomach, cradling her abdomen. The bump looked even smaller under his large hands. At five months, she wasn't showing very much, but the doctor assured her the baby's growth was right on target. "Did you hear that, little man? Mama says I get to be your daddy."

Kaytlyn hadn't known it was possible to be this happy, nor that she would see a man as tough as Cameron be so sweet and adorable. "You're too cute."

"I don't think anyone in my life has called me cute."

She laughed. "What does your mom call you?"

"Handsome," he said, pumping his eyebrows.

"I'm sure she does." She wrapped her arms around his neck, and his hands slid from her abdomen around to her back. "Handsome," she whispered, going onto her tiptoes and pressing her mouth to his.

Cameron responded—oh, how he responded—but he pulled back much too quickly. "Drink your tea; we can't be late for your appointment. We've got a plane to catch."

Kaytlyn laughed. "It's our plane, love. I think it will wait for us."

He took her suitcase in one hand and gestured to her to eat. "Okay, but the sooner we get through the doc and the shopping, the sooner I get to be married to you."

She shook her head and laughed, taking a bite of the toast and then a sip of the tea. While she didn't love the flavor, it was so thoughtful of Cameron to bring her tea and toast like he had those horrible weeks she'd been sick. She downed it without saying anything, smiling over the top of the teacup at him the entire time.

They arrived at the doctor's office, and Tyler and a redhead guy—she could never remember his name—followed them into the office. Cameron did a sweep of the patient room she'd be using and then gave her one quick kiss and said, "We'll just be in the waiting room."

Kaytlyn squeezed his hand. "Shouldn't be too long."

"Good." He nodded to the nurse and walked out, pulling the door closed behind him.

"Who's the hot military guy kissing you?" the nurse asked.

"My fiancé," Kaytlyn said proudly.

The nurse did a double take as she put on a blood pressure cuff. "Weren't you recently married and then engaged to a ... Tyler?"

Kaytlyn nodded. "It's been quite an eventful few months."

"Sounds like it."

The door swung open and Kaytlyn looked up at two men in scrubs. Neither of them was her doctor. Sometimes medical school students did rotations, but these two looked ... far too rough. The one guy had tattoos everywhere, making him look like a horrific Halloween costume. The other guy was bald and had arms like tree trunks, and there was a leering look in his dark eyes. She hated to be judgmental, but a shiver went down her spine.

The nurse had her back to the door as she finished listening for blood pressure. The men moved quickly into the small room. One brought his elbow down on the nurse's neck, knocking her to the ground.

Kaytlyn screamed, but the other one had his hand over her mouth so quickly that barely a squeak escaped. She struggled to free herself. The bald guy held her fast as the tattooed dude plunged a needle into her upper arm.

No! Cameron! Would he even know what had happened to her? Would he know how deeply she loved him? There was no doubt in her mind that Jessica had hired these men, and if the medicine they'd given her didn't kill her, she'd be dead soon anyway.

She slumped against the bald guy, and the world went dark.

CHAPTER FIFTEEN

Cameron paced the waiting room. Tyler and Jeb kept giving him smirking looks. He'd challenge them to a sparring match, but he was too happy to fight today. He had a perma-grin on that wouldn't go away, and he could hardly believe all the happiness that was his. After the doctor and shopping, he'd have a ring on his dream woman's finger, and they'd grab some lunch and hop on a plane. They were detouring to Colorado to ask her dad's permission, but then it was on to Grand Cayman. Tomorrow, he'd be married. To Kaytlyn.

The waiting seemed interminable. He perked up when he heard a shout, and he started forward. Suddenly, the doctor burst out into the waiting room and yelled, "You!" pointing straight at Cameron.

Cameron reared back, pointing a finger at himself.

"They've taken Kaytlyn!" the doctor screamed; then he turned and ran back down the hallway, and the door fell closed behind him.

Cameron's world imploded. Kayt. No! He had the presence of mind to yell, "Jeb, get the car! Tyler, you're with me," before bursting through the door after the doctor. Luckily, the nurse had buzzed it open, or he would've ripped it off its hinges.

He saw the doctor running down the hallway toward a back door. Nurses were watching in confusion. "Call 911!" Cameron yelled, pointing at the nearest nurse.

The doctor disappeared out the back door. Cameron was through it seconds after him, in time to see a black Tahoe squeal away from the parking lot.

"There!" the doctor screamed. "That's the man I saw carrying her."

As the car sailed past, a bald guy with a satisfied smirk on his ugly face tilted his chin up at Cameron. Cameron pulled his pistol out from the holster hidden on his back. He only carried when they were out of the house, but thankfully, he hadn't let his guard down today. He shot at the left tire several times, but the bullets didn't penetrate. He didn't dare shoot anything else for fear of hitting Kaytlyn. Yet if the tires were bulletproof, the vehicle would certainly be. Whoever Peter and Jessica had hired to kidnap Kaytlyn had good equipment.

Tyler was right next to him, shooting at the tires as well. The doctor cowered, covering his head with his arms.

Jeb squealed to a stop next to them in the Porsche Macan.

Cameron yanked open the passenger door and scrambled in, Tyler jumped in behind him, and Jeb floored it after the Tahoe.

Cameron's hand was shaking so badly, he could hardly transfer his gun to his left hand and retrieve his phone from his pocket with his right. His eyes were locked on the Tahoe speeding away in front of them. His stomach was clawing its way out of his throat. Focus. He needed to focus and save Kaytlyn. There was no other option, because without her, his world would end.

"Don't lose them," he said tightly to Jeb.

"Don't worry, sir. I almost made the NASCAR circuit." Jeb grinned, and the Porsche tore after the Tahoe.

Cameron dialed, and soon the call was picked up.

"911. What's your emergency?"

Cameron swallowed hard and tried to speak evenly. "My fiancé, Kaytlyn Klein—I mean, Tarbet—has been kidnapped. The suspects are in a black Tahoe, Idaho license plate, 5B 82952." They were close enough that he could squint and see it, but his grip on the phone was slipping. He'd never been so unsettled and shaky. "We are heading northwest on Warm Springs Road."

The lady tried to interrupt, but he said shortly, "The only persons who would want to kidnap Kaytlyn are Jessica and Peter Humphreys. I request you send officers to their home and offices, and any vacation properties they may own."

Cameron couldn't handle speaking anymore. He handed the phone to Tyler. "Talk to her."

Tyler took the phone, and Cameron registered that Tyler was

answering questions about who they were, how the abduction happened, and what relation Jessica and Peter were to Kaytlyn. Cameron was laser-focused on the car in front of them. Every muscle was tense, and he wanted to jump out of the vehicle and sprint to burn off some energy.

They were traveling almost straight west on Warm Springs now. The road wasn't as well-maintained and occasionally they slid on an icy spot, but Jeb was every bit as good of a driver as he'd claimed he was. They were keeping pace with the vehicle in front of them, but the men had clearly seen them and knew they were following them. Did they hope to lose them in the mountains?

The road became more twisted, snow-packed, and lined with thick trees covered in white. Cabins were dotted throughout this area, and the hot springs were nearby. Cameron kept waiting for the whine of sirens to be following them, but he didn't hear them yet.

Tyler stopped talking, and Cameron whipped around. "What?"

"Dropped the call." Tyler returned the phone, his face more serious than Cameron had ever seen it.

Cameron pushed out a breath. "They should be coming, though." But none of them had to say it. This area was remote, and that Tahoe could take any number of back roads and the police would have no clue where they'd gone.

At that moment, the Tahoe did turn off the road in front of them and sped up a winding, snow-covered dirt path. Cameron heard Jeb curse, but he spun off the road and followed them. They followed their tracks as they took several more turns. Far too much time passed as they traveled farther into the woods. Luckily, the sport utility was four-wheel drive, so it could handle the road okay.

Cameron clenched his jaw and muttered a prayer in his mind. He could hardly stand to think of his Kaytlyn in some kidnappers' clutches. He was convinced it was Jessica. It could be someone else wanting a ransom, but why did it seem like they'd almost allowed them to follow?

They wound deeper and deeper into the mountains, until suddenly they rounded a final bend. There was the Tahoe and a nice cabin, two stories, with lots of windows to take in the view of the snow-covered pine trees cascading up and down the mountainside. The Tahoe appeared deserted, and everything around the cabin looked the same, but there were tracks leading through the thick snow. Had they unloaded Kaytlyn and gotten her inside that quickly?

Cameron found himself putting a cautious hand on Jeb's arm. He wasn't sure why he didn't want to talk, as if they could hear him.

"Do you feel like we're being set up?" Tyler asked from the back seat.

"Definitely," Cameron said. "What weapons do you two have on you?"

"Nine mill and a knife," Jeb grunted.

"Same."

Cameron opened the center console of the Porsche and took out three semiautomatic Glocks. At least they'd have a backup weapon. "Back around the trees so they don't see us getting out," he instructed Jeb.

Jeb slowly reversed and parked behind some thick tree and foliage cover.

"Okay," Cameron said. "We have no idea what we're facing. I'm going in. You two take cover outside. If I'm not back out in five minutes, you find a way in."

They both nodded and silently crept from the vehicle, plowing their way through knee-deep snow, hiding in the trees as they made their way to the cabin. Cameron assessed the cabin and considered how he could best enter. Kaytlyn was in there, and it seemed like the kidnappers wanted him in there too. He was going to give them their wish and then some. He cocked his gun and started his approach.

Kaytlyn felt like she was coming out of the fog of anesthesia from the dentist's office. Her head ached, and she couldn't move. She blinked and tried to open her gritty eyeballs. A large, open room came into focus as sunlight streamed through lots of windows, almost blinding as it bounced off the snow. Beyond that was a myriad of snow-laden pine trees.

Slowly turning her head, she saw two men sitting at a table nearby. Recognition and fear rushed back quickly. Baldy and Tattoo Guy from the doctor's office. They'd drugged her and brought her to some cabin? She wanted to yell and scream for help, but from the rugged look outside, this cabin was a long way from a neighborhood. She strained to pull her hands free, but they were tied behind her.

Where was Cam? Did he even know she'd been kidnapped? Her stomach was pitching with horror as the bald guy glanced up and then grinned at her. "She's awake!" he hollered.

A door opened and a thin, blond woman strode out. Jessica. Apparently the fifty-million-dollar settlement had been too easy, a decoy. Kaytlyn took slow breaths, praying desperately and trying to act like she wasn't horrified to see Jessica here. Her former friend didn't look like herself anymore. She'd lost weight and her face was haggard and her eyes terrifyingly cold.

Jessica strode right in front of her and slapped her hard across the face. Kaytlyn's head flipped back, and pain radiated through her cheek and jaw. Jessica leaned in close, sneering at her. The hatred she obviously felt for Kaytlyn was so strong it oozed from her. "Thought you'd won, didn't you? You should've known I'd never back down. That money is *mine*. You don't deserve it." She raised her hand as if to hit her again.

"Touch her and I'll cut out your heart," a deep voice said from behind Jessica.

"Cam!" Kaytlyn yelled, relief as strong as her terror rushing through her. She strained to be free of the restraints.

Cameron stood there in the doorway, so tall, handsome, and perfect. He'd found her. No one could ever hurt her with Cameron around.

He stalked into the room with a gush of cold air, a pistol aimed at Jessica. Baldy and Tattoo Guy had sprung to their feet and were aiming their own guns at Cameron.

"Let her go and I might let you live," Cameron said.

Jessica smiled easily. She pulled out a knife.

Cameron shook his head. "Don't you dare touch her."

"I'm just cutting her free."

Cameron weighed his options, looking at each of her captors in turn. Baldy and Tattoo Guy were definitely a force to be reckoned with and appeared to know how to use the guns in their hands.

"Carefully," Cameron cautioned. "You cut her, even a tiny slice, and I'll make you wish you were never born."

Kaytlyn's heart thumped faster as Jessica came behind her and did indeed cut her hands free. She stood quickly, intent on getting to Cameron's side as fast as possible.

Jessica reached around her and held the knife right at her abdomen, stopping Kaytlyn in her tracks. A bedroom door behind Cameron opened and three men burst in. He whirled to face them, but they tackled him straight to the ground. Baldy and Tattoo Guy joined the fight, and for a moment Kaytlyn couldn't even see Cameron at the bottom of the pile.

Kaytlyn didn't dare move as Jessica held the sharp knife so tight to her stomach; she was sure that if she flinched, Jessica would cut her and hurt the baby. She watched in horror, crying out as Cameron fought valiantly, throwing one man off and into a nearby couch, slamming two men's heads into each other. She heard a crack and a shriek as he wrenched one man's arm so hard that it broke.

He sprang to his feet. A man leapt on his back and put a choke hold on him, but it didn't slow Cameron down; he spun away from the men trying to grapple with him and dropped to the ground. The man on his back took all his weight and screamed out, releasing Cam.

She'd never seen anything as impressive as him fighting, but it was five against one and these men were obviously highly trained as well. Kaytlyn screamed out as all five of them, even the one with the broken arm, jumped on him as if on cue and pinned him to the ground. Four men each grabbed one of his limbs, pressing hard to secure his body, and Baldy squatted in front of him after he was sure he was secure. Baldy whipped a knife out and held it close to his face.

Cameron stared up at Kaytlyn, his eyes filled with devotion, and then he sneered at Baldy. "Try it. Your tongue will be gone before you know what hit you."

Jessica laughed, long and low. "You're in no position to be making threats," she said.

"You'd be surprised," Cameron growled.

A look of fear crossed Jessica's face, but then the exterior door banged open and Tyler and their other security guy both walked in, followed by two more of Jessica's henchmen. Tyler and their other guy had their hands up, and each had a pistol pointed at their heads.

Worry appeared in Cameron's blue eyes; he hid it quickly, but it still set Kaytlyn's gut churning. She wanted to inch away from Jessica's knife and protect her baby, but she couldn't risk it. Seven men against their three, and they definitely had the upper hand. Kaytlyn bit at her cheek until she tasted blood, trying to hold in the scream.

"So," Jessica said. "This is how it's going to play out." She finally pulled the knife from Kaytlyn's abdomen, set it on the table, and pushed some papers and a pen toward her. "You're going to sign these papers that make me the beneficiary of all my father's assets upon your death."

Kaytlyn grunted. "You're so stupid. Nobody is going to believe I signed that voluntarily."

Jessica growled and looked like she was going to slap her again, but her gaze darted to Cameron and she stopped as she saw the palpable fury in his eyes. He was pinned down by five men, and still he looked awe-inspiring and glorious, like he was going to win this battle. Kaytlyn had no clue how, but even Jessica must have known to fear him.

Jessica whirled back to Kaytlyn. "You just inspire men to give you everything, don't you? The angelic face, the perfect body." She rolled her eyes. "First my father and now Cameron."

"Where's your scum-ball husband?" Kaytlyn challenged. "He doesn't support you?"

"Peter." Jessica sneered. "Peter can't get his hands dirty, and he has a soft spot for you a mile wide. Don't think you're special, he loves a lot of women." She shuddered. "He doesn't even know about this. He's happy about the fifty million to further his political ambitions and sad that he won't get to know his child." She glared at Kaytlyn's abdomen. "Stupid Peter is in Washington D.C., hiding his latest hooker, and he thinks I'm still in our Boise house fighting the flu—which is perfect, as my staff here also believe that lie and I've got plenty of alibis. Oh, Peter will be thrilled when I have even more money to help him on his road to the Presidency, but he doesn't want to see how I'll get him there."

She shoved the pen at Kaytlyn, and her face turned even uglier. There wasn't a trace of her former friend in that face. Kaytlyn had assumed Peter was the driving force behind Jessica's scheming. He'd probably driven her there with his infidelity and twisted sense of right and wrong, but she could see that Jessica was now dark, twisted, and flat-out crazy.

"You're going to sign this, and then we're going to burn you and Cameron alive." She smiled. "Your two security guys will be outside in the woods, just coming to when the police arrive. You'll be happy to know that they'll live, but the kerosene on their hands will prove they started the fire. Did you know this is one of *your* cabins? Nothing to tie it to me at all. I used to love coming here with my friends in high school. Dad didn't even change the pass code. It's like he wanted me to use it to burn you alive."

Kaytlyn's stomach rolled at the level of crazy Jessica had reached. She was insane. "What happened to you? We used to be friends."

Jessica let out a laugh. It was shrill and disturbing. "You were only a means to an end."

That hurt, but Kaytlyn refused to show her. She sat straighter and tilted her chin imperiously. "Tyler and J-J ..." It was something with a J.

"Jeb," the redheaded guy supplied, smiling kindly at her. Why was he smiling?

"Tyler and Jeb will tell the police everything, and the police will believe them," Kaytlyn said. "They both have impeccable records."

"Sadly, Tyler and Jeb will have taken a shot of Versed. That, combined with some Valium and their head injuries, will make them forget the past few days. They'll have no memory of any of this and no way to implicate me."

Kaytlyn thought the plan was idiotic and implausible, but she didn't bother pointing it out to her. The EMTs could find the drugs in their system. The police would have to point the finger at Jessica, no matter what alibis she had. The truth would come out. Not that it would matter to Cameron and Kaytlyn, as they'd be dead.

"Sign it," Jessica snarled.

"Don't sign it!" Cameron roared.

Jessica's hand shook slightly as she shoved the pen into Kaytlyn's hand. "Sign it or his face gets carved up."

The horror of her dream a week ago rushed over her. Cameron being tortured. Her having to watch. She couldn't let that happen.

"If you sign it," Jessica continued, "I'll simply have my men tie you both up and shoot you so you don't burn alive. If you don't sign it, they'll carve up Cameron's face, and then I'll personally carve your baby out, and then we'll burn you alive."

"How could you become this evil?" Kaytlyn asked. Her entire body shook.

"You have no clue ... Sign it!" Jessica yelled. "Or I start with Cameron's face."

Kaytlyn stared at Cameron. He smiled at her, as if everything was going to be okay. How could he be so calm and self-assured? Then his eyes slid to the knife on the table. Kaytlyn took a deep breath as Cameron roared, "Now!"

She saw Jeb and Tyler whip around, knocking the guns from their guards' hands as Cameron bucked his body and sent men flying. She wanted to watch the fight, but she had her instructions. She grabbed the knife on the table and whirled on Jessica.

Jessica shrieked and threw her hands up, backing away. Cameron launched a man away from him as Jeb and Tyler fought two men each. The man Cameron had thrown knocked into Jessica's legs, and she went down in the fray, where she was pummeled by her men as well as Cameron, Jeb, and Tyler.

Kaytlyn wasn't sure how to help as she clutched the knife and watched the men duke it out. Cameron was like a machine, punching one man, then grabbing another one and slamming his head into the wall. Kaytlyn had never enjoyed watching ultimate fighting, but seeing her man fight to protect her made something deep and warm erupt in her chest. He'd made no empty threats; that was clear as the men crumpled around him. Two were knocked out, and two were clutching their arms as if they were broken. Jeb and Tyler had grabbed guns and were pointing them at the three men who still looked like they had a little bit of fight left in them.

Jessica tried to scuttle away, but Cameron grabbed her leg and she face-planted on the wooden floor. "Stay down," he growled.

She screamed and crawled away from him.

He let her go, focusing on Kaytlyn. "Kayt. You're okay?"

"Yes." She was still clutching the knife with slick fingers.

"It's all over, love. We'll tie them up and then direct the police here."

One of the men Tyler had a gun trained on tried to dodge away while everyone was looking at Kaytlyn. Jessica dived at Kaytlyn, barreling into her legs, and the knife went flying out of her hands. Kaytlyn hit the floor and landed on her side as two quick shots rang out. She heard two thuds. Looking up, her eyes widened as she saw one of the men bleeding and either unconscious or dead on the floor. Right in front of her, Jessica was obviously dead. Kaytlyn hated what her former friend had become and how her life had ended. Pain ripped through her for the loss of someone she'd cared about and how it must've hurt Jacob to have his daughter end up like this.

The door burst open again and she heard, "Police! Hands where we can see them!"

Everyone obeyed, except for Cameron. He dodged around men until he reached her and helped her to her feet. "Are you okay, love?" he rushed out.

"Yes."

"The baby?"

"He's fine." She cradled her abdomen. She hadn't fallen on it, and right then, she felt a quick movement from within and smiled. "He just kicked me."

"Hands in the air!" the police officer commanded.

Cameron slowly lifted his hands, but his gaze stayed trained on her. "You did so good," he said. "You were so brave."

Kaytlyn lifted her hands, following his example. "I was brave? You were like some superhero, some machine. I'll never tease you about your threats again. I know you're not bluffing."

Cameron chuckled, even as police pulled his hands down and cuffed him.

"What are they doing?" Kaytlyn cried out.

"It's all procedure. They have to cuff everyone, but it's fine. They'll sort it all out."

A police officer came up and cuffed her hands as well, a little more gently. Baldy was howling in protest as they cuffed him; it looked like Cameron had broken his arm.

"It's all over, Kayt," Cameron reassured her. "It's going to be fine."

The policemen were now escorting everyone out of the cabin, at least those who weren't dead or unconscious. Kaytlyn and Cameron were escorted close together. She gave one last look at Jessica's still form, said a prayer for forgiveness, and pushed it out of her mind as they exited the cabin.

She squinted as they walked out into the sunlight, which was valiantly breaking through the thick shade of all the trees surrounding the cabin, and the snow sparkled brightly. Her baby moved again and she felt hope and the newness of life. Jacob would want her to move forward and be happy. She glanced up at Cameron. She definitely would be happy with him by her side.

"This might change our plans today," she said.

"No, ma'am." He smiled softly at her. "I am buying you the prettiest ring and dress you can imagine, and we're flying to Grand Cayman to get married."

The police officer escorting Cameron chuckled. "You've got a really positive attitude. You obviously haven't dealt with the paperwork involved after a mess like this."

Cameron shrugged. "You can expedite it for us. I've been waiting far too long to get married to this beautiful woman."

The man held Cameron's head as he helped him into the police car. "We'll try, sir, but don't get your hopes up."

Cameron winked up at Kaytlyn. "Too late. You have no idea how high my hopes are."

Kaytlyn laughed. The sunshine burst through the trees above her as the officer helped her into the other side of the vehicle. She was handcuffed and had just been through the most horrific event of her life, but Cameron seemed completely at ease, as if he already knew that everything would work out perfectly. She'd trust him, just like she always did.

CHAPTER SIXTEEN

Kaytlyn and Cameron got out of the police station a lot faster than the officer had implied they would. They had to make a trip back home to get cleaned up, but then they shopped, bought her a gorgeous diamond ring and a dress, and were on their way to Colorado by late afternoon. It was a quick flight, and Kaytlyn's eyes went back and forth between the huge round diamond on her finger and the handsome man by her side.

Before she knew it, they were waiting at her parents' front door, the evening shadows stretching long across the snow. The porch sagged and the ranch looked more run-down than she remembered. There were no Christmas decorations. When they were young, her mom had tried to do a tree and stockings, but her father had raged about the waste of money. At least the valley was as pretty as ever with thick snow covering most of the ugliness of the ranch.

Tyler and Jeb stayed in the second vehicle, waiting for them. The security might be overkill at this point with Jessica dead and Peter arrested, but it felt reassuring. Also, Tyler and Jeb were their friends now, so of course they needed to come to the wedding.

Cameron squeezed her hand, tilting up his sunglasses to wink at her. "Don't worry, love. I won't threaten your dad."

Her hands were shaking. "I'm not worried about you. I've seen firsthand your superhuman self-control."

He leaned close, bent low, and whispered in her ear, "Resisting you, a man would have to be superhuman."

She smiled and leaned into his lips.

Her mom opened the door, squealed, and threw her arms around Kaytlyn's neck, eyeing Cameron with apprehension and awe when she pulled back. She didn't invite them in. She looked so beat down and haggard that Kaytlyn wanted to cry. Kaytlyn rarely let herself feel guilty about leaving her family, but at times like this, it almost overwhelmed her. Could she have protected her mom and sisters if she'd stayed?

Her dad came storming up to the porch from the barn, obviously already in a rage. Kaytlyn recognized that staying would've destroyed her like it had her mom, unless it drove her to drugs like it had Kandy. Where was Krysta? Kaytlyn couldn't care less about her dad's permission; she'd come here to try to rescue Krysta and her mom.

Her father's eyes lingered on her abdomen, and he started ranting. He obviously already knew about the baby. "You knock my daughter up and then think you can come here and get my blessing?" he yelled, but Kaytlyn noticed he stayed about twenty feet away from them, lingering on the snow next to the porch.

Cameron remained calm as he faced her father. "Sir, I would like your blessing, but I don't need it. The baby isn't mine, but I will raise him as my own and love him and your daughter with every part of me."

Her dad's eyes narrowed at Kaytlyn. "The baby isn't even his? It's that old guy's, right? The guy you were a hooker for? What kind of a whore have you turned into?"

Cameron released her hand and marched down the porch steps and right up to her father, bearing down on him as her dad faltered. He ripped his sunglasses off and said in a low voice, "I have lived in conditions so miserable that they make this squalor of a home look like a palace. I have tolerated pain, discomfort, gunshot, and knife wounds, but I will never tolerate you speaking to my Kayt that way. Apologize ..." His voice rose. "Now!"

Cameron stepped back as if to give him room to apologize, and possibly to keep himself from hitting him.

Her dad glared at the porch swing and said, "I'm ... sorry."

Cameron must've realized her father was a lost cause, because he walked back up the porch steps, extended his hand to her mother, and graciously shook her hand. "It was very nice to meet you. Please let us know if there is anything we can do for you." He glanced back at her father, who was glaring daggers at him but immediately dropped his gaze when Cameron looked at him. "Kayt?" he said softly. "Are you ready to go?"

"Yes." She gave her mom a hug and murmured in her ear, "We can help you."

Her mom squeezed her tight but shook her head. "I'm fine."

Kaytlyn didn't believe that, but she couldn't force a grown woman who had never stood up for herself to stand up to her husband. Her sister was a different story. "Where's Krysta?" she asked quietly.

"Krysta's gone. She's working," her father said gruffly.

Kaytlyn didn't even want to address him. "Where?" she asked her mother.

"In town, at the ice cream shop," her father said.

She looked up to Cameron. She didn't believe her father; he'd never let them work anywhere but the farm. How was she supposed to call his bluff?

Cameron bent down close and whispered in her ear, "We'll find her."

"Thank you." She took Cameron's hand, and they walked off the porch and toward the gravel drive as if they were going to leave. They couldn't leave. She needed to explain to Cameron that her dad was lying and Krysta was probably out in the barn or sheds.

They were almost to the rented Audi when Kaytlyn heard pounding footsteps and a yell of "Kayt!"

Cameron shielded her body with his, but she pushed at him and exclaimed, "Cam, it's my sister!"

He stepped to the side but still overshadowed her, and it was clear from his body language that he wasn't going to let anyone hurt her.

"Kayt." Krysta's steps slowed as she stared from Kaytlyn to Cameron. She was in worn-out clothes, but she was clean and she had the face of an angel. Kaytlyn opened her arms, and Krysta hurried to hug her. "I've missed you!"

"You too." Kaytlyn turned her sister toward Cameron. Her parents hadn't moved, and she ignored her dad's glare and her mom's worried gaze. "This is my fiancé, Cameron Bodily."

"Hi." Krysta appeared almost shy, and with a pang, Kaytlyn wondered if she was beaten down like their mom. Krysta had always been a rambunctious, funny child. Kaytlyn had hoped she'd follow her example and leave, especially since she and Jacob had tried to get her to leave three years ago. She had to know she could come to them, but she never had left.

Krysta's eyes darted from their father to Cameron; then she whispered to Kaytlyn, "He's really tough and hot."

"That he is." Kaytlyn winked at her fiancé. It was amazing to think that word in relation to Cameron. Finally.

Her dad stormed away back to the barn and her mom shrank into the shadow of the porch.

Kaytlyn grabbed both of Krysta's hands and lowered her voice. "Come with us."

"Where?"

"We're flying to Grand Cayman right now and getting married tomorrow."

Krysta backed away. Her eyes darted to the barn. "Dad would kill me," she muttered.

"Krysta. You're twenty years old. You can do what you want. I've been texting you since you turned eighteen, offering to come get you and have you come stay with me."

Her sister shook her head. "Dad took my phone a long time ago. I never saw your texts."

That sent red-hot rage shooting through Kaytlyn, and she clenched her fists. So her dad had been pretending to respond to her as Krysta? What a low-lying piece of scum he was. "It's time," Kaytlyn said decisively. "Come with us."

Krysta worried her lip, but her blue eyes lit with excitement. "I've never been anywhere."

"Let's go."

They looked back at the house. Mom was still in the shadow of the porch, but she nodded decisively. "Go." Then she spoke in a quieter voice, as if afraid their father would hear: "Don't come back, love."

Krysta ran to the porch and hugged their mother tight; then, just as quickly, she scrambled into the back seat of the Audi, slamming the door shut and putting her seat belt on. She looked like a little girl thrilled to go on an adventure.

Kaytlyn wished they could haul her mother out of here too. She gave her one more pleading look and said, "Please, Mom."

Her mom shook her head, pulled the door to the house open,

and slipped inside. So she wanted them to save Krysta, but she still wouldn't take the opportunity to save herself.

Cameron's eyes were flitting between the house and Kaytlyn. "I'm sorry, Kayt. I don't know that we can force her."

Kaytlyn sighed. "No, but we won't give up."

"Okay." He tucked some hair behind her ear, and his voice dropped. "Will your father hurt her?"

"Not physically. He'll throw a temper tantrum and pout and punch holes in the wall, but he was more about controlling us with his anger and his words than ever laying a hand on us." She looked back at the house, wishing she could rescue her mom. After thirty-plus years of marriage to a controlling jerk, her mom might never be free. At least they had Krysta with them now.

Cameron walked around the car with her and opened her door, escorting her into its welcoming warmth.

Krysta was almost bouncing with excitement in the back. "This car is sweet. It's almost as pretty as your fiancé."

Kaytlyn laughed, relief rolling through her. She ached for her mom, but she couldn't change her decisions. For now, she would have fun being around Krysta and enjoy every minute of her wedding and honeymoon. "Don't say that around him. He thinks he's too tough to be pretty."

Cameron opened the driver's side door and climbed in as Krysta pretended to zip her lips. Her sister was still as adorable. Kaytlyn was so happy, despite having to leave her mom again.

He smiled at them. "Are you ready to go to the most amazing wedding of your life?" he asked.

Krysta nodded vigorously. "I'm ready to go wherever you say. Are you rich?"

Cameron threw back his head and laughed, starting the vehicle. "It's your sister that's rich. I'm just her arm candy."

"You did not just say that." Kaytlyn laughed as they pulled away from her family home. She didn't let herself look back and feel sorrow for her mom. She looked ahead, to a future with Cameron. The wedding was going to be amazing, especially with Krysta there. The honeymoon would be even better. She settled her hands over her sweet baby and felt the little guy kick.

"She's my sugar mama," Cameron said.

"Good for you." Krysta laughed. "And you're having a baby?"

"Yes. It's going to be a boy," Kaytlyn said.

"You don't know that," Cameron said.

"Yes, I do, and I'm naming him Jacob."

Cameron slid his sunglasses on and reached over, taking her hand. "We'll see, love. We'll see."

"Yes, we will."

EPILOGUE

The wedding was more amazing than Kaytlyn could have dreamed, and the honeymoon exceeded her every expectation. The devotion, passion, and love she felt for and from Cameron were unequaled. She'd worried about entertaining their families in Grand Cayman, but Krysta had become fast friends with Cameron's sisters, who enjoyed flirting with Jeb and Tyler and being on a tropical vacation. She and Cameron had almost enough alone time, and his family was amazing, especially his mom, who instantly adored Kaytlyn.

When they got back to Sun Valley, everything with the businesses, the charities, Christmas, and the house were busy and demanding as ever. Kaytlyn thrived on it, though, especially with Cameron working alongside her. He might have been one of the most impressive security guys she knew, but he could also run a business with grace and talent, and they were great partners.

Peter was arrested briefly but sadly released. The good news was his political career was ruined by Larry's allegations. His party dropped his bid for senate and he seemed to have disappeared. Kaytlyn was just thrilled she didn't have to see him again, and she still blamed him for destroying Jessica.

They bought a little house in town, and they spent almost as much time there as they did in the mansion. It was fun to be together, just be the two of them. It was great to have Krysta around too, when she wasn't in Ohio with Cameron's family; the girl was flourishing and had decided to start school at Ohio State in the fall. They sent lawyers to Kaytlyn's parents' house with money and with offers for her mom to come visit. They were turned away every time. It hurt, but they decided to keep trying.

Her due date, April tenth, came and went, and she could've sworn her body couldn't stretch any farther. Cameron took such good care of her, always bringing her different herbal teas that were supposed to be good for the baby. He claimed she was the most beautiful women ever, but she knew she was swollen and gargantuan. She'd more than made up for all the weight she'd lost at the first of the pregnancy. She probably looked as miserable as she felt.

Finally, on April fourteenth, the doctor induced labor. Kaytlyn wanted to go natural, but after ten hours of contractions, the only thing in her life that had felt as good as that epidural was Cameron's touch. He stood stoically by her bedside, trying to anticipate her every need, holding her hand, feeding her ice chips, and smoothing back her hair.

After twenty hours, she was finally dilated to a ten and the doctor blessedly said it was time to push. Twenty minutes later, a squalling, red-faced baby covered in white mucus joined the world.

"It's a girl," the doctor said happily, holding the baby up for them to see.

"It's a ... what?" Kaytlyn stared in happy, exhausted confusion. She'd been so certain the baby was a boy.

"A girl?" Cameron's face lit up. The joy in his blue eyes made Kaytlyn grin.

They wrapped the baby up in a warm blanket, and the nurse rubbed a white substance off her face before they handed her directly to Kaytlyn. Kaytlyn cuddled her against her chest, bursting with rightness and joy. "A girl." She shook her head, staring in awe at the beautiful, wrinkled face. The baby had Kaytlyn's lips, but beyond that, she couldn't say who she looked like.

"A girl," Cameron repeated happily. He wrapped his arms around both of them. "I'm so happy right now."

"I thought you wanted a boy."

Cameron shook his head. "I wanted a baby with you. I don't care if it's a boy or a girl."

"But we were going to name him Jacob."

Cameron chuckled. "The next baby will have to be Jacob." He gazed at their daughter with love shining in his blue eyes. "I didn't know it was possible to fall head over heels in love as fast as I did with you."

Kaytlyn smiled. "That's why it took you two years to ask me out."

"Hey, I'm a slow military man. Be nice."

The doctor delivered the afterbirth and the nurses were waiting to weigh and check the baby, but nobody really interrupted them.

"So, Jacob won't work ..." Kaytlyn pursed her lips. "Jacqueline, maybe?"

"Nah. The next baby will be Jacob," he said stubbornly. "This one needs the name of a princess. She's going to be as beautiful as her mama."

Kaytlyn leaned into him and said, "Okay, my military man. What is it, then?"

"Isabella, and we'll call her Belle," he said decisively.

"I love it." She cuddled back against his chest, tilting her head up to smile at him.

Cameron bent close and gave her a lingering kiss. "I just love you."

Kaytlyn held her baby close and snuggled against her husband. She'd never been so blessed, and she was going to raise this baby with all of her love. The anguish that she and Cameron had gone through to get here was definitely worth it.

ABOUT THE AUTHOR

Cami is a part-time author, part-time exercise consultant, part-time housekeeper, full-time wife, and overtime mother of four adorable boys. Sleep and relaxation are fond memories. She's never been happier.

Join Cami's VIP list to find out about special deals, giveaways and new releases and receive a free copy of *Rescued by Love: Park City Firefighter Romance* by clicking here.

Read on for a quick excerpt of the first book in Cami's Strong Family Romances: *Don't Date Your Brother's Best Friend*.

cami@camichecketts.com
www.camichecketts.com

DON'T DATE YOUR BROTHER'S BEST FRIEND

Ella Strong drove her new Camry down the mountain pass that led to her Colorado valley and sighed with relief, "Home." The little town of Lonepeak was all there like a postcard in front of her. Downtown still boasted wide tree-lined streets and quant little shops, all cookie-cutter with a faux wrought-iron railing on the second story and their own light post. Houses and farms were spread throughout the valley. Honest, hardworking people she'd known and loved her entire life occupied those spots just like she'd remembered—and, in her mind, just as they should be.

She strained for a peek at the spot she loved most in all the world, without running her new car off the road. There. Straight across the valley, she could make out the lodge rising above the pine trees, with ski lifts and runs twisting up the mountain behind it. In June, the lifts were used for mountain biking instead of skiing, but she loved that too.

The Strong family had owned and operated Angel Falls Retreat since before Ella was born. Her mama's family roots were here, and they'd owned the property and a small ski lift and bed and breakfast. Her parents had met snow-skiing in Aspen as college students. They'd both dreamed and schemed of making the mountain into something incredible. Many years and hours of work later, it was a thriving year-round retreat. Her oldest brother, Gavin, mostly ran the resort now. Ella's second-oldest brother, Heath, had even expanded the concept and had resorts of his own in Utah, Wyoming, Connecticut, and West Virginia.

Ella pushed the pedal down. The car responded, and she bypassed town and made it home in record time. She pulled into the main lodge parking lot. There were smaller villas scattered away from the main lodge, and the newer spa and ski and bike shop was to the east. Her family's home was west, in a smaller canyon. Their canyon was private and gated, hidden from the resort, but she knew Gavin was a workaholic. She'd find him here and maybe Austin and Mama, then go see her papa.

Sliding into a parking spot, she jumped out and hurried toward the lodge. A man whizzed through the parking lot on a mountain bike. He must not have seen her, as he almost buzzed her.

"Watch out!" Ella called.

"Excuse me," he said, braking to a stop. He spun around and pedaled back to her. Stopping right in front of her, he leaned over his handlebars. His eyes swept over her, letting her know he was interested, but it was a little over the top. She didn't even know him, yet he gazed at her like he had paid for the right to gawk. "I wasn't paying attention to where I was going."

"Apparently," she sassed back, putting one hand on her hip and tossing her long, dark curls.

He grinned. "Can I gain your forgiveness by buying you dinner?"

Ella took a quick inventory, not sure if she wanted to spend more time with this guy or not. He was a built dude and his bike was top of the line, Emonda. His high-end bike clothes reeked of wealth. Not that she was opposed to wealth, as long as the guy had earned it. Hardworking and fun were qualities at the very top of her list for the man who would snag her heart.

"No, you can't," a voice said at her shoulder.

Ella knew that voice. She loved the depth and timbre of it. Quite often, she heard it in her dreams. She turned slightly, and there he was. Trey Nelson. The man who had defined everything that she'd wanted in a man since the day she'd realized boys and girls were different creatures.

Unfortunately, Trey had never wanted her in return. He was the best friend of her oldest brother, Gavin, and since he was six years older than her, Trey had always treated her like his little sister. He was protective of her, liked to tease her, and had probably never once envisioned dating her like she dreamt about daily. Correction: used to dream about.

She was a successful college grad now, all finished with Stanford and three months into her first job, a marketing specialist at a fabulous start-up company based in Salt Lake City. They specialized in electronic billboards and were growing like mad. Her job was to get them even more contracts, and she was killing it, if she did say so herself. Her boss seemed pleased, and she enjoyed the work, though the sprawling Salt Lake valley was too populated for a backwoods girl like her. She'd come home for Labor Day weekend to enjoy family and her mountains, and then she'd be back to the real world. At least the mountains east of Salt Lake had some great hikes and bike paths she could escape to after work and on the weekends, after she navigated through traffic for a miserable hour.

"I think the lady can decide for herself," Rich Guy said.

"Back off, Marcus. This one's mine." Trey's eyes swept over her, and for a second, she really thought he meant it, really wanted her to be his. Then he acted like the annoying, possessive big brother, putting his hand on her lower back and escorting her toward the lodge without giving her a chance to choose for herself. She'd choose Trey every time, but she was an independent woman and he needed to know that.

The Richie—Marcus, she supposed—grunted something annoyed and not very appropriate behind them, but Ella was having a hard time focusing with Trey's warm palm on her back, seeping through her thin shirt, and his words. "'This one's mine'? What kind of bull crap is that?" she asked.

Trey smiled down at her, but his blue eyes had something different in them than she'd ever seen. It was almost like he was finally seeing *her*, but that was probably just wishful thinking on her part. "It'll get that loser to leave you alone. He's with a corporate retreat out of Denver, and most of them are stand-up guys, but Marcus Traegger thinks he owns the world and every woman in it."

"Maybe I prefer guys like that." She arched a challenging eyebrow. The truth was that no man had ever compared to Trey, but he didn't know that. Hopefully, he would never know that. How humiliating would that be?

He opened the lodge's door and ushered her inside. "I'd say too bad for you, because Gavin and I are *not* letting it happen." He glowered down at her. It was odd to see anything but a smile on Trey's handsome face. He was just one of those contagiously happy people. Add to that his good-looking face with the slightly longer curly golden-brown hair and the bright blue eyes she couldn't resist and she could understand why every woman flung herself at him. No matter how jealous it made her.

Ella stopped just inside the door, taking in the huge open room welcoming her and a pretty blonde she didn't know manning the front desk. They were far enough away that they still had a small measure of privacy. She whirled on Trey, ready to give him a piece of her mind. He had plenty of women after him, and she could choose if she wanted to go to dinner with some rich yahoo.

A deep voice said, "What aren't we letting happen?"

Ella pushed away her frustration with the bossy, too-handsome Trey and turned. Her oldest brother, Gavin, was striding down the grand staircase as if he owned the world, or at least owned this corner of it. He pretty much did, though her mama still had her hand in everything. From what Ella had seen on her brief trips home, Gavin was taking over more and more. He was brilliant at it, though it had always baffled her that he'd never left the valley. He'd had a full-ride scholarship to Texas A&M, planning to play cornerback and get his undergrad before going on to law school. Ella had only been twelve at the time, so her memory was a little fuzzy, but she did remember her parents going from thrilled and proud to withdrawn and sad. Papa's accident had happened around the same time, so Gavin never went away to college; he just got his degree online and worked night and day to make the resort even better than anyone could've dreamed. Stetson, their twenty-year-old brother, was fulfilling Gavin's dream, playing defensive end for Purdue and making everybody proud.

"Gavin!" Ella rushed to the stairs.

He met her at the bottom and lifted her off her feet, swinging her around. "Hey, Cinderella," he teased. "Come home to clean the chimney?"

"Yes, sir. Put me to work, big brother."

He released her from the hug and looked her over. "You're too pretty to be working."

"That's what I thought," Trey said from behind her.

Ella caught a glimpse of a warning in Gavin's eyes before she rounded on Trey. "Like you'd ever look at me as anything but a sister," she hurled at him.

Trey's eyes widened, and she almost faltered. The color of his eyes could go from teal-blue to a more true blue depending on what he was wearing or his mood. His eyes had always mesmerized her.

"He'd better not," Gavin growled. He wrapped an arm around her shoulders. Protective and in charge of everybody, that was her big brother. She adored him, but she quite often balked at him telling her what to do. She was very unlike her twin, Cassandra, who was obedient and sweet. If Trey had any inclination to realize she was a woman, she didn't want Gavin scaring him away.

Trey said nothing, and that frustrated her even more. So he gave a secondhand compliment, but then when she called him out, gave him the chance to say he didn't think of her as a little sister anymore, he clammed up. What did she expect? She'd been around Trey all of five minutes, and of course she'd imagined something different in his eyes; she'd been praying to see a glimmer of interest for years. The fact that he'd probably never see her as anything but a little sister made her want to punch him in the gut, but that was unfair. This was all on her.

"What are you doing here, anyway?" she demanded of Trey. "Don't you have Instagram videos to shoot for your admirers to gawk over?" Trey was an Instagram and YouTube hotshot. He made videos showing and instructing how to do insane, border-line idiotic tricks on mountain bikes and snow skis. Ella followed him. How could she help it? But she'd noticed that most of his followers seemed to be female and were enthralled with his perfect face and tough body more than learning how to do any of his tricks. She didn't blame the women, but she could still admit it annoyed her.

"I hired him," Gavin said.

"You can afford him?" Ella asked. It sounded more like something their brother Heath, would do. His four resorts were even more lavish than this one, and he was always doing some kind of interesting promotion.

Trey chuckled. "I gave him a discount."

Gavin cracked half of a smile. "You'd better not have, you idiot."

Trey just gave them a self-satisfied smirk and stepped closer. "To answer your question, beautiful Cinderella, Gavin hired me to impress a bunch of corporate yuppies who have booked the resort this weekend to teach them tricks so they can impress their friends when they go home."

"So you're only here for the weekend?"

"Not long enough for you?" Trey arched an eyebrow.

No, it would never be long enough for her. She'd be happy to spend the rest of eternity with Trey, but she clamped a lid on that fantasy. Trey was no Prince Charming, and she was better suited to clean the chimney than campaign for Trey's affections. Judging by the way he appeared to flit from one gorgeous woman to the next, she should be glad he wasn't interested. He'd reel her in, maybe finally kiss her like she'd always dreamed about, and then he'd dump her and move on. She'd be in a worse position than ever.

Keep reading here.

ALSO BY CAMI CHECKETTS

Strong Family Romance

Don't Date Your Brother's Best Friend

Her Loyal Protector

Steele Family Romance

Her Dream Date Boss

The Stranded Patriot

The Committed Warrior

Extreme Devotion

Quinn Family Romance

The Devoted Groom

The Conflicted Warrior

The Gentle Patriot

The Tough Warrior

Her Too-Perfect Boss

Her Forbidden Bodyguard

Georgia Patriots Romance

The Loyal Patriot

The Gentle Patriot

The Stranded Patriot

The Pursued Patriot

Jepson Brothers Romance

How to Design Love

A Touch of Love: Summer in Snow Valley

Running from the Cowboy: Spring in Snow Valley

Light in Your Eyes: Winter in Snow Valley

Romancing the Singer: Return to Snow Valley

Fighting for Love: Return to Snow Valley

Other Books by Cami

Seeking Mr. Debonair: Jane Austen Pact

Seeking Mr. Dependable: Jane Austen Pact

Saving Sycamore Bay

Oh, Come On, Be Faithful

Protect This

Blog This

Redeem This

The Broken Path

Dead Running

Dying to Run

Fourth of July

Love & Loss

Love & Lies

Cami's Collections

Steele Family Collection

Hawk Brothers Collection

Quinn Family Collection

Cami's Military Collection

Billionaire Beach Romance Collection

Made in the USA
Lexington, KY
06 December 2019

58257435R00109